Amélie Rives

Tanis, the sang-digger

Amélie Rives

Tanis, the sang-digger

ISBN/EAN: 9783743381971

Manufactured in Europe, USA, Canada, Australia, Japa

Cover: Foto ©Andreas Hilbeck / pixelio.de

Manufactured and distributed by brebook publishing software (www.brebook.com)

Amélie Rives

Tanis, the sang-digger

TANIS,

THE

SANG-DIGGER

BY

AMÉLIE RIVES.

NEW YORK:
TOWN TOPICS PUBLISHING CO.,
21 WEST 23D STREET.
1893.

TANIS, THE SANG-DIGGER.

CHAPTER I.

GILMAN was driving along one of the well-kept turnpikes that wind about the Warm Springs Valley. He recognized the austere and solemn beauty that hemmed him in from the far-off outer world; but at the same time he was contrasting it with the sea-coast of his native state, Massachusetts, and a certain creeping homesickness began to rise about his heart.

In addition to this, he had left his delicate wife suffering with an acute neuralgic headache, and also saddened by a yearning for the picturesque old farm-house in which he had been born, and where they had lived during the first year of marriage.

The trap which Gilman drove was filled with surveying instruments, and, as he turned into the rough mountain road, which led towards the site of the new railway for which he was now pros-pecting, the smaller ones began to rattle together and slide from the seat beside him. Finally, as the cart slipped against a stone, the level bounced into a puddle. He was about to jump out when a bold, ringing voice called to him:

"Set still—A'll pick hit up!"

Then a figure slid down the rocky bank at his right, her one garment wrinkling from her bare, sturdy legs during the performance.

Gilman had never seen anything like her in his thirty years of varied experience.

She was very tall. A curtain of rough, glitter-ing curls hung to her knees. Her face, clear with that clearness which only a mountain wind can bring, was white as a sea gull's breast, except where a dark, yet vivid pink melted into the blue veins on temples and throat. Her round, fresh

lips, smooth as a peony-leaf, were parted in a wide
laugh, over teeth large and yellow-white, like the
grains on an ear of corn. She wore a loose tunic
of blue-gray stuff, which reached to the middle of
her legs, covered with grass stains and patches of
mould. Her bare feet, somewhat broadened by
walking, were well-shaped, the great toe standing
apart from the others, the strong, round ankles,
although scratched and bruised, perfectly sym-
metrical. Her arms, bare almost to the shoulder,
were like those with which, in imagination, we
complete the Milo. Eyes, round and colored like
the edges of broken glass, looked boldly out from
under her long black eyebrows. Her nose was
straight and well cut, but set impertinently.

As she picked up the muddy level she laughed
boisterously and wiped it on her frock.

"Thank you," said Gilman, and then, after a
second's hesitation, added:

"Where are you going? Perhaps I can give
you a lift on your way. Will you get in?"

"Well, a done keer ef a do," she said, still
staring at him.

She got in and took the level on her knee, then burst out laughing again—

"A reckon yuh wonders what a'm a haw-hawin' at?" she asked, suddenly. "Well, a'll tell yuh! 'Tis caze a feels jess like this hyuh contrapshun o' yourn. A hain't hed a bite sence five this mawnin', and a've got a bubble in th' middle o' *me*, a ken tell yuh!"

She opened her flexible mouth almost to her ears, showing both rows of speckless teeth, and roaring mirthfully again.

"I've got some sandwiches, here—won't you have one?" said Gilman.

"Dunno—what be they?" she asked, rather suspiciously, eyeing him sidewise.

He explained to her, and she accepted one, tearing from it a huge semi-circle, which she held in her cheek while exclaiming:

"Murder! hain't that good, though? D'yuh eat them things ev'y day? Yuh looks hit! You're a real fine-lookin' feller—mos' ez good-lookin' ez Bill."

"Who is Bill?" asked Gilman, much interested

in this, his first conversation with a genuine savage.

"Bill? he's muh pard, an' muh brother, too. I come down hyuh tuh git him a drink o' water, but a hain't foun' a spring yit."

"No, there isn't one in several miles," said Gilman.

"My Lawd above us!" she cried. "Hyuh! Lemme git out. Whar be yuh agoin', anyhow?"

Gilman told her.

"I've an idea," he added. "If you'll wait for me here, I'll be back in about an hour, and I'll bring you some water."

She turned on him, her brow knotted into a fierce frown.

"Ho! *I* knows yuh!" she cried. "You're one o' them stuck-up valley fellers. *I* knows yuh! You're ashamed tuh git caught ridin' wi' me!"

"Indeed, I'm not," he said, flushing.

"Yuh *air!*" she retorted, angrily. "*I* knows yuh! You're one o' them fools ez reads books, an' thinks nothin' 'live's got any sense but yuh-selves. But yuh's jess ez big a fool ez anybordy!

A hain't thought yuh looked suh *pizen* smart fum
th' fust. Yuh got nice shiny har an' eyes, an' a
sweetish mouth, an' these hyuh fool things ez yuh
go 'long th' road a-droppin' fur other folks tuh
pick up. Thar! hit'll sarve yuh right ef hit
breks," and, with a jerk of her strong wrist, she
sent the level flying over the horse's head.

Being unaccustomed to having levels hurled
about her ears, the mare snorted and reared, half
whirling around at the same time.

"Sit still!" cried Gilman, sharply, as the girl
was about to jump out. "What a vixen you are,
eh?" he added, good-naturedly, as he pulled up
the mare in order to get his unfortunate instru-
ment.

"Will you hold the reins, Mademoiselle, while
I pick up my 'contrapshun' this time?"

"Hyuh! done yuh call me no names," she replied, threateningly. "A've licked Bill lots o'
times, an' a lay a ken lick you."

"Mademoiselle only means Miss, in French,"
explained Gilman, meekly.

"Then you call me 'Miss,' in English," she

growled, surlily. "That's some more o' yo' stuck-up foolishness. 'Sides, that wud didn't soun' like it was Miss, in no langidge. Hit sounded like a red-hot cuss wud, an' a wone stand no more on 'm."

"Bill must have a calm, sweet life," suggested Gilman, mildly, getting in with his level.

"*Yuh* let Bill alone," she snapped back. "He'll scalp yuh, quickern' a Injun, ef yuh fools wi' me."

For about a mile they drove on in silence; then, at the edge of the wood, Gilman pulled up.

"Now," he said, "you may get angry again, but I'm going to say to you what I'd say to my own sister. First, I don't want to take you any further, because we'll soon be among a lot of rough men, white and black. Second, I want you to tell Bill that I don't think he ought to let you scramble about these lonely woods, by yourself, with only that one piece of clothing on."

"Now, *you* look a-hyuh," she retorted, narrowing her eyes upon him. "Ef you want me to war more cloes, you jess start about an' get 'em fuh

me.   Bill hain't got no money tuh wase on sech
darn foolishness."

"Very well," said Gilman, "I will, with pleasure.   If you'll come home with me, I'll give
you some, to-day.   By the way, will you tell me
your name ?"

" *You* tell me yourn."

"My name is George Gilman."

" Well, mine's Tanis.   Funny kynd o' name,
ain't hit ?"

"It's very like the name of a Carthaginian
goddess."

"A Carthagi—now, you look a-hyuh ! Done
you begin yo' book-stuff on me agin—a wone
stand hit."   She brought her fist down so
energetically upon her crossed knee that her leg
flew out as if moved by machinery.

"Yuh hyah me ?" she said.

"It's very hard not to make you angry,
Miss Tanis."

"No 'tain't, nuther, ef yuh talk sense tuh
me.   But a nuvver could stand Torm fools,
not even muh ole dad ; he was one," she

added, quickly. "A nuvver did see whar Bill an'
me got our sense, case Ma, she wuz one, too."

Gilman got down hastily, to hide a smile,
and turned to give her his hand, but she was
out, with the bound of a deer, before he could
touch her.

"You g'long," she said; "a'm sorry a rode
this far wi' you. You'll larf 'bout muh bar
foots, an' this hyuh rag o' mine, wi' them po'
white trash an' niggers. Whar you fum, anyhow? Yuh hain't a Fuginia feller. A kin tell
by yo' talk. You called roots 'ruts' jess now,
an' yuh said we'd 'sun' be whar them other
fellers be. Whar you fum?"

"From Massachusetts," said Gilman.

"S'that another langidge fuh some name a
knows?"

"No—it's the real name of another State."

"Well, hit's 'nuff tuh twis' a body's tongue,
fuh life, so a done blame yuh s'much fuh yo'
funny talk. Mawnin'." And she began to
swing herself upon a great lichen-crusted boulder by the roadside.

"Then you're not going to wait and go back with me for the clothes?" asked Gilman.

"Mebbe a will, an' mebbe a wone. A'll do ez a darn please; yuh ken gamble on thet."

"Well, good-bye, then, Miss Tanis. I suppose you won't tell me your last name?"

"Muh lars' name but one's Gloriany.' A've got three," and she grinned at him.

"But the other?"

"Nuvver *you* mine," she called back, from her perch far above his head. "M'other name's ugly 'nuff tuh give Satan th' toothache. But that hain't no odds. We gals ken alluz change our names. Now yuh g'long an done drap that cussed old bubble agin, or hit'l bust, sho'."

She gave a wild whoop of laughter at her own wit, and was soon out of sight, in the thick woods.

CHAPTER II.

GILMAN was naturally curious as to the type of young barbarian whom he had met on his drive to Back Creek, and, during a pause in his work, he told a young fellow named Watkins of his adventure, and asked him to what class the girl belonged.

"I reckon, sir, she was a sang-digger," said Watkins, laughing. "They're a awful wild lot, mostly bad as they make 'em, with no more idea of right an' wrong than a lot o' ground-horgs."

"But what *is* a 'sang-digger'?" asked Gilman, more and more curious.

"Well, sir, sang, or ginseng, ez the *real* name is, is a sorter root that grows thick in the mountains about here. They make some sorter medicine outer it. I've chawed it myself for heartburn. It's right payin', too—sang diggin' is, sir; you ken git at least a dollar a pound for it, an' sometimes you ken dig ten pounds in a day,

but that's right seldom. Two or three pounds a
day is doin' well. They're a awful low set, sir,
sang-diggers is. We call 'em 'snakes' hereabouts,
'cause they don't have no place to live 'cep'in' in
winter, and then they go off somewhere or ruther,
to their huts. But in the summer and early au-
tumn they stop where night ketches 'em, an'
light a fire an' sleep 'round it. They cert'n'y are a
bad lot, sir. They'll steal a sheep or a horse ez
quick ez winkin'. Why, t'want a year ago that
they stole a mighty pretty mare o' mine, that I set
a heap by, an' rid off her tail and mane a-tearin'
through the brush with her. She got loose somehow and come back to me. But they stole two
horses for ole Mr. Hawkins, down near Fallin'
Springs, an' he a'in't been able to get 'em back.
There's awful murders an' villainies done by 'em.
But some o' them sang-digger gals is awful pretty,
though they go half naked in summer time an'
are mostly mighty dirty. Yes, sir, I reckon she
was a sang-digger, shore enough."

Late that afternoon, as Gilman reached the
big boulder up which the girl had climbed that

morning, a loud halloa stopped him, and, looking up, he saw that she was swinging herself down its fern-tufted sides.

He pulled up and waited to see what she would say.

Coming close to the side of the cart she put a bare foot on the step, and stood looking at him for a while in silence. Her hair rioted as freely as ever, but she had thrown a bit of bright crimson stuff about her shoulders, and a man's soft hat, ornamented with a deer tail, was pulled down about her ears.

"Say!" she burst forth, finally. "A was pizen mean tuh yuh this mawnin'. A reckons yuh done keer 'bout totin' me back fur them duds?"

"Why, yes, I do," said Gilman, pleasantly. "Jump in."

She hesitated for a second, and then bounded in beside him, shaking the whole vehicle and starting the mare into a gallop. After another second she addressed him, with her usual explosiveness.

"Be yuh a-doin' o' this hyuh outer cussedness, or be yuh a-playin' on the squar'?"

"What do you mean by doing it out of 'cussedness'?" asked Gilman.

"A means, be yuh a-goin' tuh yank me off somewhar an' keep me, or be yuh agoin' tuh give me them duds an' lemme go? A reckons a'm a darn fool tuh go wi' yuh — *that's* whut a reckons a be."

"Why, of course I'm going to let you go," he said, smiling.

"Then a reckons *you're* a darn fool, too," was her brief comment. "They been't a feller, wi' any gumption under his hat, t'wix hyuh an' the Blue Ridge, ez 'ud lemme go onct he got a holt o' me. But a hain't nuvver hed a feller yit," she added, quickly. "When they tries thar fool tricks wi' me a smacks 'em upside down." She looked at him steadily for a moment, and then said, with slow. emphasis:

"No feller hain't nuvver kissed me sence a wuz bawn, 'cep'n Bill. D'yuh b'leeve me, or d'yuh think a'm a blamed liar?"

"I believe you," said Gilman.

Her eyes softened.

"A reckons you're th' right sort," she said, smiling. "A reckons *you're* a gentleman."

"I have thought so," he returned, also smiling.

"D'yuh know what *I* be?" she demanded, after another period of silence. "Well, *I* be a sang-digger. They calls us 'snakes,' them valley fools does. We're a right wile lot, too, stranger. No feller ez done want daylight through him, oughn't tuh monkey wi' no sang-digger, man or woman."

"No," said Gilman, gravely. "I should think not."

She regarded him again with silent intentness, and then observed, deliberately:

"There was a sang-digger onct murdered a man fuh twenty cents. I've biled coffee fuh him many a time. He wuz a right kynd sorter feller, too, Jim wuz; but he hed a drunk on, an' he wanted that twenty cents. A knows whar th' other feller's skellington is now, but a wouldn't tell yuh ef yuh cut ma th'oat fuh it. Jim wuz th' kyndest feller tuh dumb critters yuh ever see in yo' life. A tole him ef th' man had been deef an' dumb he wouldn't a stuck him. Hit didn' seem to bother Jim, though.

He said he hed to tell *somebordy*, so he tole me;
then he felt fust rate. He said ez how th' man
heddn't but one leg, ennyhow, an' a feller wi' only
one leg wuz better off whar he wouldn't need *no*
legs. He said he'd thank anybordy tuh put a hole
through *him* if *he* didn't hev but one leg. An' he
spent that thar twenty cents on whisky, an' drunk
hit, too ! Jim wuz a caution, but he never fooled
wi' *me*."

Gilman gazed at her, with a certain blankness of
expression. He wondered what the writer of Ec-
clesiastes would have said about her.

Her next remark showed a sudden change of
thought.

"This hyuh rag a got 'round muh neck's a right
prutty color, hain't hit?" she asked. "Bill tore
down a lot o' winder things outer a woman's house
lars' winter, an' *I* tuk *this* hyuh one, an' dyed it
with pokeberries. Hit sots off ma har right well
—done it ?" And, pulling one of her heavy tresses
over her shoulder, she began to curl it around
her fingers, and spread it out on the gaily-colored
stuff.

It suddenly occurred to Gilman that he might have some trouble in explaining this young woman to Alice, who was always interested in the poor people whom he brought home, for employment or aid.

"Did yuh ever see har no prettier nor mine?" she then demanded.

"No; it's very beautiful, and you've got such a lot of it," said the young man.

"We be reel chummy, muh har an' me," she went on. "When hit tuns cold in th' mountains, a wrops hit 'round me, an' hit kynder comforts me. A nusses hit on muh bres, like a baby, sometimes. An' a talks tuh hit. Seems like hits a critter, all tuh hitself, muh har does. Sometimes hit wone skars curl, tuh save muh neck; then, agin, hit twangles up, mos' like a nigger's, an' hit done stay th' same color two days han' runnin'. Mos'ly hit's like hit is now, but sometimes hit's percisely like raw wood in the sunlight, when them little red, shiny flames is beginnin' tuh lick roun' hit. Hit's got streaks in hit, too, mos' zackly like a new silver quarter. See?" And she pulled it back from her temples and turned her head aside, that he might look.

Somehow, Gilman felt very glad that dusk was beginning to gather, so that his companion was somewhat veiled from the passers-by. He felt that he had caught a Tartar with a vengeance, and the idea of Alice, confronted with this wild mountain girl, disturbed him more and more.

When he reached Fern Ledge, as they called their house, he asked Tanis to hold the mare, while he went for some one to put her up. This was, however, only a subterfuge, to get a chance of explaining the situation to Alice. He found her recovered from her headache, and marking a copy of Shelley's poems, the covers of which were beginning to curl from being held so near the fire. She smiled at his fears, and told him to bring the girl to her at once.

When Tanis entered, she stood for a moment, blinded by the white glare from the two lamps which lighted the pretty room, although the sun had not quite set. Then, brushing her hand across her eyes, she advanced a step or two and then stood still.

It was a simple little picture—the graceful, high-born woman half rising from her sofa, the tall, embarrassed man, with his pronounced air of civilization, ushering in this wild creature, clothed about in her web of wind-snarled hair—the little room, bright with white and blue chintz, with bowls of flowers, with water-color drawings, its cottage piano littered with music, its low tables friendly with books! There was a warm scent of Russian leather and roses in the air.

Tanis was the first to speak. She looked paler in the white lamplight.

"S'that yo' woman?" she demanded, briefly, pointing to Alice.

"That is my *wife*," said Gilman.

"She looks a heap older'n you do," remarked the girl.

"I *am* older," remarked Alice, gently, a pink spot painting itself under either eye.

"Well," observed Tanis, "*I* holes ez how th' man oughter be the oldest. Now, when *he*,"

jerking her thumb towards Gilman, without looking at him, "when *he's* a good-lookin', middle-
aged feller, *you'll* be all tuh pieces."

"My husband loves *me*, not my looks," said
Alice, her face tingling, as though from a smart
blow.

"My!" muttered the girl, "hit's mighty hard
tuh tell how much hit's *looks* an' how much hit's
ooman a man loves. *Looks* is got a heap to do
wi' *love*, a kin tell yuh! You're right nice-lookin'
now, but you're mortal skinny, an' yo' eyes swivel
when yuh smiles, a-ready. Yuh awful little, too.
A feller could lose yuh twix' his shirt-collar an'
his ves'-porket, an' nuvver know whar yuh went
tuh. Hit cert'n'y do beat me why you two got
hitched. Wuz she rich?" she ended, turning to
Gilman, whose face was flushed and angry. He
was in a horrible position, fearing to oppose her, lest
she should grow violent, and seeing, by his wife's
face, that each brutal word was a home thrust.

"I think you said something about clothes,
George," said Alice, coming forward. "I will go
and get them."

He went out with her, supporting her with one arm, and Tanis was left alone in the fragrant room. She wheeled about, and scowled at the closed door.

"Well, of all the two-legged Jack-asses!" she said, at last, in her slow growl. "Well, of all th' darn Torm-fools!"

She brought her hand down, with a bang, on the object nearest her, which happened to be the piano. The shrill discord startled her, and she leaped back; then, venturing to approach it again, struck some single notes with her forefinger. The sound displeased her, however, and she turned away, lounging about the room with her free, woodland motion. She opened a book or two, wet her finger and touched the lamp-chimneys cautiously to see if they would "smack;" pulled out the pictures from the wall, in her desire to know if the colors went through to the other side, and, finally, opened Alice's bottle of crown-lavender salts, which she had been using for her headache.

"Murder!" she cried, as Gilman entered, fling-

ing it from her, so that it smashed on the slate
hearth, "the cussed thing's wuss'n a gun.   A
thought muh head wuz off."

" Here are the clothes," he said, drily.   " There
is a bedroom across the hall where you can put
them on."

She stared at him.

" Wut's the bed got tuh do wi' hit?" she then
demanded.   " Does yuh wooman git in bed tuh
dress herself?"

" It isn't necessary to mention my wife," he
said, tartly.   " A bedroom is the place where
people usually put on their clothes."

" Well, a hain't a-goin' in no bedroom," she replied, looking obstinate.   " A'll put 'em on hyuh,
or a wone put 'em on nowhar."

" Very well," said Gilman.   " I'll go out until
you are ready."

Again she stared at him, and then burst into her
tempestuous laugh.

"Lawdy, lawdy!" she cried, " but you valley
fellers air a caution!"

She came to the door in a few minutes, and

called to Gilman, who was pacing miserably up and down the hall.

"Say!" she shouted, "how many o' these hyuh duds *be* thar, *anyhow?* A hain't got room on me fuh any mo', an' ther's 'bout three lef' over."

"Make them into a bundle and take them with you," he said, distracted.

"Well," she assented, "a mus' be a-movin', too. Bill, he's a-goin' tuh meet me over tuh Rourke's. A reckon a kin light out up th' mountain from hyuh, cyarn't a?"

"But you'll tear your clothes all to pieces," he objected. "I haven't unhitched the mare. I'm going to drive you to the place where you told me your brother was going to meet you. You can't scramble through the brush with these clothes on."

"A hain't *gwine* tuh," she said, briefly; "a'm gwine tuh tek 'em off th' fus' fence a comes tuh."

"Of course you can do as you like," he replied; "but I'd much rather drive you, if you don't mind."

She stood still and looked at him curiously.

"*Hed* you ruther?" she asked, in a gentler voice.

"Yes, much rather. It's really horrible to think of a woman's wandering about these hills alone at this time of the evening."

Her whole face had softened. The bold eyes regarded him almost shyly.

"Stranger," she said, " hit's reel kynd o' yuh tuh think 'bout that."

With a sudden movement, she came nearer him.

" A'm sorry a spoke so tuh yuh 'oom—yuh wife. A lay a hut her, right smart. A'm sorry. Tell her a'm sorry. A'll mek Bill bring her a lot o' fustrate sang. She looks like she needed some sorter doctor stuff. A'm sorry."

Gilman could not have believed that he would ever forgive her, but something in the wild, wistful eyes touched him.

"Yes, I'll tell her," he said, and put out his hand.

She touched it, half timidly, then stroked it with her finger-tips.

"Hit's ez smooth ez sang root," she said, finally.

Then, lifting her eyes to his, "A likes yuh."
Then, lifting her face, " Yuh ken kiss me, ef yuh
keers."

Gilman's embarrassment returned tenfold. He
smiled, and said with an effort:

" Do you know, Miss Tanis, I like to think that
no man has ever kissed you—not even myself.
But I'll kiss your hand, if I may." And he lifted
the rough, shapely fingers to his lips.

"Somehow," she murmured, her lips working
nervously—"somehow a feels like a reckon other
'oomans feels when they're a-goin' tuh cry. A
done nuvver 'member cryin'. Hit huts muh
th'oat." She turned from him and walked
abruptly out into the solemn, evening atmos-
phere. The blackish violet of the hills made a
sombre outline against a pale sky where, through
streamers of dim red, the stars were beginning to
shine. No words were exchanged between them
until they reached Rourke's, where a tall, slouch-
ing figure came toward them from the shadow of
the roadside. Tanis leaped out, and, taking her
brother by the hand, drew him forward.

"Bill," she said, "a wants yuh tuh thank that—
that gentleman—he *air* a gentleman," she added,
quickly, as Bill gave a dubious grunt. "He's
ben good tuh me, an' guv me all these hyuh duds.
A wants yuh tuh look at him good, caze a wants
yuh alluz tuh stick tuh him ef uvver you'ze by an'
he gits in a tight hole. Ken yuh see him?"

"Be yuh gone silly, sis?" growled her brother.
"A feller couldn't see th' Ole Boy hisself this time
o' night, 'thout he come a-blazin'."

The girl darted forward eagerly.

"Yuh got a match?" she asked, "caze ef yuh
hev, scratch hit, so's Bill ken see yuh. 'Tain't
a-goin' tuh hut nobordy tuh hev a sang-digger
fur a *frien'*, though hit *mought* tuh hev one fur a
enemy."

Gilman reached mechanically for his cigarette-
case, and lighted the fuse.

The three faces were painted against the background of gloomy mountain by the faint, bluish
flame.

The two men looked each other in the eyes.

"A'll know yuh anywhar now," said the sang-digger, finally, "an' thank yuh fuh yo' kyndness tuh muh leetle gal. She's ez wile ez a hawk, but moughty good-hearted. She's a good gal. Thank yuh."

Gilman snapped down the lid of his cigarette-case, but the sang-digger's powerful head, with its mat of dark-red hair and beard, and gleaming, black eyes, seemed still to look at him from the curtain of the twilight.

"Good-night," he said, taking up the reins.

"Good-night," returned Bill.

"Say 'suh' tuh him," whispered the girl.

"Good-night, suh!" called the big fellow, obediently.

And the girl's voice repeated like an echo:

"Good-night, suh!"

CHAPTER III.

THE Warm Springs Valley is a long, fertile trough, extending between two spurs of the Alleghany mountains, rich in various ores and in numberless medicinal springs, whose tepid waters curl in clear, shallow brooks, through field and forest, reflecting the changeful sky with jewel-like effects, and bordered by rankly-clustering growths of water-cress. The hills are steep, severe in outline, perforated with caves, and covered by forests, chiefly of oak and chestnut, which have been much injured by frequent fires.

The shrill tang of sheep and cow bells accentuates the silence overhanging this lonely dale, varied sometimes by the crackling detonation of a rifle far up among the rocky heights.

Its peace is almost too solemn to be soothing, its beauty too severe to bring with it that sense of closeness which possesses us in the presence of rare, natural scenery. It has in it something of that chill which emanates from a woman whose loveliness is too haughty to be magnetic. One has a sensation of mountains, piled up on all sides in countless ranges, like gigantic walls which seem to shut out the world beyond and even love itself.

From the top of the Warm Springs mountain one can count five or six ranges to the northward, sweeping on and on, like the petrified waves of a once liquid and stormy sea of sapphire.

It seems hallowed for the cradle of a severe and narrow region. The dryads of its trees one fancies to be nuns, and the genii of its caves, brown-cowled monks, imprisoned there for crimes long since forgotten by the far-away world. The Titans, held down by these masses of iron ore and sandstone, must have been the rebel Gods of a Methodistic heaven. The hot water, welling everywhere from the fat loam, brings with it suggestions of that fiery region, where the souls of the unrighteous and unorthodox are supposed to descend after death.

The very cattle seem awed by the vast impressiveness about them. One rarely hears the bleating of sheep or the lowing of cows. The locomotive,

that arrives once a day at the Hot Springs sta-
tion, does not give vent to the unmannerly snort-
ings and shriekings which distinguish other locomo-
tives.   It comes and goes, with a sombre rumble,
as if its metallic soul were subdued within it by the
general hush of hill and valley and overhanging
sky.

In spite of her absolute devotion to her husband,
Alice Gilman could not help being saddened by this
stern and imprisoning landscape.   The sound of
the sea, which from childhood had lulled her in
moods of mental and physical pain, was ever in
her ears.   She felt a heart-thirst for its open radiance, its darting gulls, its ships which seemed like
messages from the lands that she had never seen,
but of which she had dreamed during many an
hour of calm imagining.   The crowding mountains
suffocated her.   There was, for her, a gloom in the
very sunlight as it rested drowsily on the fields, not
shaken as by the restlessness of the ocean, which
she so loved.

She was leaning on her elbow at an open window
one day, about two weeks after her interview with

Tanis, her heart full of that listless pain which is born of resignation, when a voice close by startled her.

She looked up and saw that Tanis herself was standing a few feet off, leaning on a rough staff of hickory, and regarding her with the intent gaze which she remembered so well.

"Mawnin'," said the girl; then tapping a bunch of contorted roots, which hung at her side :

"A've come tuh bring yuh them sang-roots a promised yuh."

"Thank you," said Alice, nervously, half rising. Her face was already flushed, and she looked about her uneasily. "Thank you," she repeated.

Tanis advanced a step nearer.

"Done git skeered," she said, gravely, "a hain't a-goin' tuh hut yuh."

"Oh! no — no, certainly," murmured Alice. "I'm very much obliged to you. It's very kind of you."

Tanis now came up to the window and laid the roots on the ledge.

"Yuh looks better by daylight," she said.
"That's funny, but yuh duz. Yo' *har* cert'n'y
is prutty."

"Do you think so? It's very nice of you
to tell me. You must have walked a long way.
Won't you have something to eat and drink?"

"A'll tell yuh pres'n'y," answered the girl,
bluntly. "We'll see how you and me gees, fust.
Yo' *rings* air moughty prutty. 'S that yo'
weddin'-ring, all by hitse'f?"

"Yes."

"It's right narrer—"

"Yes, but it will last, I think," said Alice,
smiling. Something in this smile struck the
girl.

"Yuh be reel weakly, be n't you?" she asked,
in her softest voice. "Hit lays on yo' mind,
done hit?"

"I'm not strong. It must be wonderful to
be strong and healthy, as you are."

"Me? *I* hain't nuvver had a day's sickness
in muh life. Ain' that a arm?" And, rolling
up her loose sleeve, she thrust out for Alice's

inspection an arm as hard as gutta-percha and as white as the lining of a horse-chestnut burr.

"Feel hit," she urged. "Hit's most ez big ez Bill's." Alice pressed it timidly with her thin fingers.

"My glory!" cried the girl. "A'd be 'fraid muh han's 'ud brek off, ef a hed them wrisses! But they cert'n'y *air* prutty, though. What shiny nails! Duz you grease 'em?"

"No. I rub them sometimes with a piece of chamois leather, but not often. I don't like them to look *greasy*," and Alice observed her delicate hands closely, with an air of discontent.

"Say," cried Tanis, suddenly. "A'll tell yuh what a come for. 'Twarn' jess the sang. 'Twas tuh ax yuh suppn'."

"To ask me something?" said Alice, again nervous.

"Yes. Be yuh wantin' anybordy tuh wuk 'round th' house, or yard? A'm strong an' healthy, like yuh said. A'll wuk hard an' mine whut yuh tells me."

"I — I have all the people that I need, I think," stammered poor Alice, "but I'll ask Mr. Gilman."

Tanis waited a moment, studying the pale, lovely face of this woman who wore "city duds," and hairpins in her smooth hair.

"Whut yuh reckon he'll seh?" she asked, finally.

"I don't know," replied Alice. "Won't you come in and rest?"

"A'll come in, sho 'nuff. But a done know what *tired* means. A got on them duds yuh guv me—all 'cep'n th' wais'. *Hit* wuz too narrer. A could'n' breathe."

The next moment she entered, looking down rather apprehensively at her bare feet.

"A'm a-bringin' in a lot o' dus'," she said.

"Oh, never mind," Alice answered, cheerfully, determined to overcome her instinctive aversion to the girl.

"It's a very easy carpet to sweep. Shall I get you a glass of milk and some biscuits?"

"A hain't hongry, thank yuh. 'S'that *yo'*

baby?" pointing to a photograph on a table, near by.

Alice flushed.

"No—it's my sister's. It's a pretty little thing —isn't it?"

"*Right* prutty. A've seen pruttier. ' *V'you* got any?"

"No," said Alice, flushing still more deeply.

"Ben ma'h'ed long?"

Alice's eyes began to move restlessly from door to door.

"I've been married two years," she said.

"An' yuh ain' got a baby? Done yuh husbun' take on 'bout hit?"

"My husband is all that I could wish," replied Alice, haughty, in spite of herself.

"Well, done git mad," said the girl, calmly. "A didn' mean nothin'. Mos' mens gives they 'oomans fits, ef a baby done come 'long inside a yeah. Hit beats me, too, caze mos'ly they's pizen mean tuh 'em, arter they gits 'em. A knowed a man—Dick Senster. He had a drunk on, an' he got mad at his little gal an' roasted her foots at

th' fire an' then kilt her. They lynched him—
they did, an' sarve him right. That's true.
D'yuh b'leeve hit?"

"Oh, how horrible," murmured Alice, faintly.
" Do such things really happen about here?"

"These hyuh hills hain' no Sunday-schools,"
was the sententious reply, "but they bee'n't many
o' th' boys ez bad ez Dick wuz. They'll be
moughty mad at me, though, fuh comin' hyuh tuh
git work. But Bill, he wuz glad. We bee'n't
like th' others, Bill an' me bee'n't. Our Ma wuz
mortal silly, but she war good. She wa'n't a sang-
digger, an' Pap, he didn' tun sang-digger twell
arter he got so bu'nt up wi' whisky he couldn'
shoe hawses. A hain' nevver cyar'd on wi' th'
boys. Fust place, Bill 'ud a kilt me—seckint
place, a hates mens, all cep'n Bill. A hates low
talk, an' a hates low doin's. Wan' me tuh tell
yuh supp'n? Well, a come down hyuh to see
how hit feels tuh be wi' decent folkses. A reckon
hit'll war me out, arter a while, but a'm a-goin'
tuh try hit, ef yuh'll lemme."

Alice had an almost morbid sense of duty

toward every creature that crossed her path. She
held out her slender hand, and said, quickly:

"Let me be your friend. You can help the
cook, and I'll teach you to sew."

Tanis looked at her, with a touch of the old
suspiciousness.

"Yuh tuns 'bout right quick, doncher now?"
she said, dryly. "Thought yuh hed to wait tuh
ax yuh man—yuh husbun', a mean?"

"I'll have to do that, too, of course," replied
Alice, controlling her indignation and still holding
out her hand, "but we generally agree."

Tanis took the slim fingers gingerly into her
own.

"A reckon yuh're right spiled," she said,
slowly. "A reckons he does whut yuh wants,
prutty puncshul. Yuh're the *kynd* men spiles,
though. A feels like sorter nussin' yuh up
muhse'f. Yuh puts me in mine uv a squrl a hed
onct, wi' a broken foot. A could lif' yuh 'bout
like a baby. Say, yuh done like me fur *nuthin'*—
does yuh now?" she ended, explosively.

"Oh, no—no, indeed!" cried Alice, more crimson than ever. "I mean I have only the kindest feelings for you. Why should you say such a thing?"

"Kin see hit in yo' eyes," said the girl, briefly. "But nemmine, a reckons a'll suit yuh. A'm nach'lly clean. Doncher come down on me too hard at fust, though. A've got a temper."

CHAPTER IV.

THE people of the neighborhood were loud in their ejaculations of horror and condemnation when they heard that Mrs. Gilman had taken a "snake" to help her in general housework. Tanis, however, proved that she was thorough and willing in her work, and, during an illness of the cook, took her place to Alice's entire satisfaction. She now wore a plain, but well-fitting gown of dark gray stuff, her hair was braided and coiled at the back of her handsome head, her shoes of stout cowhide were neat and fitted her, and her round ankles were covered with stockings of dark gray yarn. She would not have anything to do with the people about the Hot Springs, and was, as a rule, rather silent.

One day Gilman approached her as she was crossing the backyard, on her way from the cow-pen, her strong figure swayed to one side by the heavy pail of milk which swung from her reddened hand. She stopped and looked at him questioningly.

"I'd like to talk to you a few moments," he explained. "I've been wanting to say something to you for several days."

"Well?" she answered.

"We're afraid—Mrs. Gilman and I—that you're lonely here," he went on. "Haven't you made any friends in the neighborhood that you'd like to see sometimes?"

"Nuck," she replied at once, with her usual brevity. "They's mostly pizen fools ez lives 'bout these parts. You'd take a sang-digger fuh President 'longsider 'em."

"But you must be very lonely in the evenings."

"Naw, a been't, nuther. A'm larnin' that thar punch-wuk Mis' Gilman showed me howter do."

"Then we both think you work too hard."

She began to look obstinate.

"Reckon a knows how much a ken wuk and how much a cyarn't, t'hout other folks hevin' tuh tell me. Reckon yuh'd better lemme tend tuh *my* wuk an' *you* tend to *yo'n.*"

"But, my child, you're thinner than you were. Really, we can't let you overwork yourself."

"A hain't yo' chile, 'n' a hain't thunner, 'n' a hain't overwuken muhse'f."

"We're afraid that you're unhappy, and won't say so for fear of annoying us."

"Naw, a hain't, nuther. A'd gnaw yuh swif' enough ef a hed any call tuh. Don' *chu all* bother 'bout me. *A'm* all right."

Two hours later, however, as she was chopping some lightwood for Alice's bedroom fire, the supply having suddenly given out, and there being no one else to do it, her name, uttered softly in a man's voice, caused her to pause, axe in air, her face going from white to red, from red to white.

"Tanis! *Tanis,* muh prutty!" called the rich, pleasant voice again.

She faced about, her arms tense, the axe still held above her head.

"Sam Rose!" she said, in a stifled, throaty voice. "By th' Lawd above, a've a good min' tuh fling this hyuh axe stret at yo' head!"

"Fling hit, muh honey." he whispered back, smiling. "Put me outer torment, an' a'll thank yuh fuh hit."

She lowered the axe slowly, trembling as she did so.   Her face grew whiter, her eyes fixed themselves upon his.   Then she began to walk, hesitatingly, step by step, toward him.   When she reached the fence, upon which he was leaning, he jumped over, and caught her in his arms.   She stood there for a moment, without expression or movement, but, as he began to bend her head backward and reach his lips to hers, she flung him from her, so that, giant as he was, he staggered, and caught at the fence for support.

"Oh, yuh blackguard, yuh!   Yuh low-down blackguard, tuh try tuh hut me wi' these hyuh folks ez is so good tuh me!   Some day a'll tell Bill on yuh, an' he'll cut yo' heart out!"

She stood panting and staring, but he did not attempt to touch her again.   No, he smiled, show-ing white teeth, regular and animal as a dog's, and began to pull at his short, blond beard, which gave him the air of a young Zeus.   It was, indeed, astounding how complete a Greek the fellow looked, in his ragged flannel shirt and rough cowhide boots.   He must have stood at

least six feet five in his stockings. His nose and
forehead were as Phidian as anything in the Vati-
can ; his eyes a laughing, dazzling, shallow, for-
get-me-not blue, his hair and beard a bright, crisp
gold. He ended by laughing, and said, in reply
to her last statement regarding his heart :

"Ef he doez, he'll hev tuh make a hole in *yo'*
breast, fuh that's whar 'tiz, beauty, sho !"

She stood quite still, her body bent back, her
hand extended in front of her, and tensely
clenched.

"Hain't yuh larned yo' lesson yit ?" she said, in
a low voice. "Hain't yuh got no pride ? Hain't
yuh got nothin' of th' man 'bout yuh, but yuh
strongness ? A didn' know even a bawn sang-
digger cud git so low ez tuh be alluz a pesterin' of
a gal ez hev tole him over a million times how she
hates him !"

Again he smiled.

" *Yuh* done hate me, honey. Aw no, *aw* no,"
he murmured, still smiling, and carding out his
beard with his great fingers. "Yuh *loves* me, a
tells yuh. Hit's like break-bone fever, love is, 'n't

goes harder wi' some 'n wi' others.   Hit's upsotted
yo' brain, muh prutty, that's all.   Come hyuh an'
lemme *show* yuh how yuh loves me."

He made a step toward her, stretching out his
arms, but she darted back, with a fierce gesture,
and picked up the fallen axe.

"Ef yuh touch me agin, a swar a'll kill yuh,"
she panted; but he only gave another of his musi-
cal bass laughs.

"By Gawd, yuh looks prutty when yuh're mad,
honey!   A hain't nuvver hed sech a thust on me
furrer gal sence a cud tell sang from pizen-oak;"
then, with a sudden change of tone, "drop that
axe—drop hit, a tell yuh!"

She grasped it all the tighter, and gazed at him
defiantly, but, little by little, her fingers loosened
from about the haft, her eyes began to waver, her
face grew pale and set; she let the axe fall at her
side.

"A clar tuh grahus, yuh'd make a *meek*, *'bejent*
little 'oman, yuh would," he said, resuming his
lazy, half-sneering tone of good humor.   "A've a
mind tuh mek yuh kiss me, fo' th' Lawd, a hev.

Doncher wanter heah a song a made up 'bout yuh, larst night?"

Leaning carelessly against the fence and keeping his eyes upon hers, he began to drone out, in a soft, glutinous bass, the following ditty:

> " Her ha'r 'tis like th' sumac,
>   Her eyes is bluer'n ice,
>   Her mouth's like partridge berries,
>   Oh, would'n' hit tase nice !
>   My Lawd!
>   But would'n' hit tase nice !
>
> " Her ankles is keen an' swif' ez a deer's,
>   She moves like a pine in th' win',
>   But ef yuh tried tuh hug her, boys,
>   She'd cuss yuh quicker'n sin—
>   She would—
>   She'd jaw yuh wuss'n sin."

He was beginning on another verse of this primitive doggerel, when Tanis, as it were, wrenched her eyes from his, and scudded into the house, before he could remonstrate with or stop her.

He only laughed, as usual, however, and taking a short pipe from his pocket, began to press down the shreds of tobacco into its bowl with one broad, yet handsome thumb.

"A'll hev her yit!" he said, addressing his pipe, gravely, before putting it between his teeth. "A'll hev her yit, or bust!"

CHAPTER V.

EARLY that evening, as Alice was half dozing on her sofa, near the fire, she heard a door open softly, and Tanis came in, on tiptoe.

"I'm awake," said Alice. "Do you want anything?"

"Ef yuh bcen't too tired," admitted the girl, hesitatingly.

She came over and stood before the fire, for a moment, and then asked abruptly:

"Ken a sot down on th' flo'? A've a heap o' things on muh mine. A lay yuh're a moughty good 'ooman. A reckon yuh ken he'p me."

"I'll do all in my power, I promise you," said Alice, cordially. She was beginning to like Tanis.

"An' yuh wone think a mean tuh sass yuh, ef a ax yuh some right pinted questions?" inquired the girl, wistfully.

"No—certainly not," said Alice, a little apprehensive, but determined to be kind.

There was silence, for quite a long time. Then Tanis remarked that the fire was "treading snow."

" What does that mean ?" asked Alice.

"Hit means we're goin' to hev bad weather—
snow, mos' likely."

Alice shivered, and drew her fur coverlet higher.

" Oh ! I'm sorry," she said. "I thought that
summer was almost here."

"This hyuh's a ondependable climick. Yuh
cyarn' nuvver tell whut day arter tuhmorrer's
goin' to be. Say—" she broke off, still staring
deeply into the flapping blaze, " say—one thing a
wants tuh ax yuh is 'bout love. Yuh'se seen a
heap o' life, 'n' yuh'se a lady—whut is love, anyhow ?"

" What is love?" repeated Alice. "Why, that
is about the hardest question in the world to
answer ! People are always asking it, and the
answers never seem to satisfy them. Different
people love so differently."

" But when a 'ooman loves a man, an' a man
loves a 'ooman, that's mos'ly th' same, hain't hit ?"

"Ah ! no," said Alice, dreamily. "That love
varies more than any other. What I call love,
some one else might not think love at all."

"Well, what does *you* call love?" asked the girl, eagerly.

"I hardly know how to put it into words. It is something deep, still, strong. Something that draws you higher—that leaves you with sweet, happy thoughts, which you almost grudge sharing with your own heart. It is rest, contentment, fulfilment, satisfaction — a reality that comes after many dreams—dreams that have perhaps been brighter, more vivid, but not half so beautiful."

"Ud that sorter love mek yuh ache tuh let a man kiss yuh, an' yit feel like yuh'd kill him ef he did?"

"Oh, no! that's dreadful," said the other, quickly.

"Ud hit mek yuh think 'bout a man, an' honger arter him, day 'n' night, an' yit long to git away fum him th' minnit yuh seed him?"

"No—no! how can you ask?"

"'T'wouldn' mek yuh think sometimes like p'raps sin wi' him 'ud be better nor goodness 'thout 'im—'ud hit?"

"Never! That isn't love. Love is goodness. Love is—"

"Well, nemmine 'bout whut love is now; jess tell me, ef yuh ken, whut that other thing is, caze thet's whut's a-wearin' me out, body 'n' soul."

Alice hesitated a moment, and then said, slowly:

"That is—is fascination, infatuation."

"A done know them wuds," put in Tanis, with disappointed bluntness. "Cyar'n' yuh mek hit plainer?"

"I will try. To fascinate anybody is to have a sort of power over them; against their judgment —their reason. You've heard of a snake charming a bird, haven't you?"

The girl started to her knees.

"A've seed hit!" she cried. "A've seed hit muhse'f. Hit air like that, sho' 'nuff!"

She sank back again, fixing her large, glowing eyes upon Alice.

"Then that thar whut a tole yuh been't love?" she asked, under her breath.

"No, never!"

"But why do hit mek yo' heart pain yuh so?

Why does yuh be alluz wukin' on that man, in yo' mine? alluz, alluz, *alluz*, day-time an' night-time? Why ken yuh seem tuh feel him sometimes a holdin' uv yuh, an' a kissin' yuh, an' hyuh his voice in yo' yeuh, like he wuz right by yuh, an' he mebbe thirty mile away? Why ken yuh see his eyes a lookin' at yuh, so bright, outer th' dark? Gals ez hev been in love hev tole me they hed them feelin's. Why be it love wi' them, an' not love wi' —wi' somebordy else?"

"I can't explain, exactly," answered Alice, "but perhaps a good woman might be fascinated, in spite of herself, by a bad man. Then she might have some such feelings."

"Oh, he *air* a bad man!" cried Tanis, passionately. "A know'd three gals he ruined. They warn't bad gals, nuther. They warn't sang-diggers. They war jess plain mountain-people, but they war hones' gals till he met 'em. One uv 'em drownded herse'f, an' they ole Grandad druv th' other two away tuh th' city. Po' things! A reckon they be low 'nuff by this time. A reckon God'll mek hit right hot fuh thet ole scalliwag uv a Grandad o' thern! Dontchu? They war all three frien's. A seen Mag, arter she was drownded. A cyarn't nuvver git her face outer muh mine." She stopped, shuddering heavily, and, pressing her eyes with her hands, a sob broke from her.

"Tanis," whispered Alice, her hand caressing the bent head. "Tanis, dear child," she repeated softly, "I wish I could comfort you—I wish I could help you. I know what heart-pain is; I have had it, too."

Tanis's first instinct was one of savage resentment, but, looking up, she met those soft, gray eyes, full of tears. Her strong brows quivered, and the next minute she was sobbing, with her head against Alice's knees. She did not say anything more, however, and Alice asked no questions, but from that hour the girl showed a rough, curious sort of affection for her, which displayed itself, sometimes humorously enough, in an outburst of jealousy against Gilman.

"A cud cy'ar yuh upstars ez good ez he cud," she would protest; "an' he wone nuvver lemme tech yuh. Folks ud think a wuz pizen!"

But, in spite of her irritability on this point she had also a sincere devotion for Gilman himself.

"'Pears tuh me," she observed one day to Alice, "yo' husbun' cert'n'y do tek arter th' Lawd. A done blame yuh fuh harf wusshuppin' him. A'd blame yuh a darn sight mo' ef yuh did'n'."

CHAPTER VI.

IT was about four o'clock one Sunday afternoon that Tanis went for a scramble on the
Warm Springs Mountain.

The soft air was perfumed with May, the dusky
hills powdered with the varying green of young
leaves. Between them the valley coiled, like some
emerald-skinned python, absorbing the slant sunlight. She reached a fence which ran along one of
the steepest flanks of the mountain, almost directly
opposite to the Hot Springs, and, noting a group of
oaks and chestnuts, thought that it would be a
pleasant place to rest for awhile, and practice upon
what she now termed " thet thar cussed punch-
wuk." Climbing over, she went toward the trees,
and then stopped short, with a look of astonishment and distaste. For, between the gnarled roots
gaped a jagged hole, some eight feet in diameter,
and descending, apparently, into the bowels of the
earth. She clutched one of the oaks firmly, and
swung her head and shoulders over the opening.

Its black wedge split the ground below her, as far
as the eye could see. Juts of sandstone roughened
its sides, and it was shaped like a huge funnel.
The girl continued to hang over it, fascinated.
Extending one hand cautiously, she lifted a loose
stone and flung it in. It bounded from wall to
wall, with a sharp noise which grew ever less, as it
descended deeper into the cavern, until at last she
could no longer hear anything.

"My! But thet u'd be a nice place tuh stumble
inter to'ds dark," she said to herself, smiling, but
with rather pale lips. "A allus did hate them thar
caves, anyhow, an' a cave a-standin' on hit's head's
a right cuss'd-lookin' thing. A wonders whar hit
goes tuh?"

As she uttered the last words she felt strong
hands grip her about the waist, and then, tearing
her from the tree, as though she had been a squirrel, they held her out above the ugly chasm.

She turned white, but did not utter a sound.

"Wanter go find out?" asked the sweet, mocking voice that she so dreaded. Still she said nothing. He gave her a little shake, as he held her,

and her ball of white crochet-cotton was shaken
from her apron pocket and fell, reeling out, yard
upon yard, until at last the thread was stopped by
a snarl, and her work itself was drawn slowly forth
and fell after the ball.

"Promise tuh kiss me, an' a'll let yuh go!" he
demanded.

She was silent.

"Wone yuh promise?"

"Naw," she said, deliberately.

"S'posin' a drops yuh inter thet thar hole, ef
yuh don't?"

"Yuh kin drop me inter hell, but a wone kiss
yuh. Drop away, an' be darned tuh yuh, yuh
coward!"

He gave a laugh and a whistle together and set
her upon firm ground, still keeping one hand on
her shoulder, however.

She was trembling, but more from rage than
fright.

"Now, hain't yuh a wild-cat?" he asked, taunt-
ingly. "D'yuh know yuh're th' fust gal ez ain'
flewed tuh me when a axed her furrer kiss?"

Tanis looked at him, contemptuously.

"Yes, 'n' much luck hit brought em, th' po' fools!"

He shook her slightly again.

"Darn my hide," he exclaimed, "but you're a natchul cu'yosity, same ez the Natchul Bridge. Why! Tarnation, honey! What's outer fix wi' muh mouth? Ain't a got nice teeth? What yuh got agin' kissin' me? Ef a had tushes, like Tommy Mings, orrer hause-tail furrer mustash, like lame Joe, yuh mought fuss, but blame me ef a ken mek out whutcher balks so at. Say," he went on, changing his tone, as he saw that this style of appeal was not having a happy effect upon her, "say, honey-gal, a loves yuh, fo' Gawd a loves yuh! Doncher know a cud hole yuh an' tek a kiss anytime a'd a mine tuh?"

"Well, why doncher?" she asked, eyeing him dangerously.

He looked down at her with an air of calm meditation.

"Caze," he replied, slowly, "a reckon yuh'll think a'm a all-fired liar, but th' truth be this: a

wants yuh tuh kiss me uv yuh own free will, an'
a'll mek yuh do hit, too, some day !"

"A'll cut muh th'oat fust !" she cried, with passion.

"An' yet, honey," he went on, placidly, "yuh
loves me. A nuvver made a slip-up in all muh
life bout a gal's lovin' me. A *knows* yuh loves
me, but why yuh be suh darned stan'-off wi' me,
well, t'ud tek th' ole Scratch hisse'f tuh settle thet
thar. An' yuh hain't 'feard o' me, nuther," he
added. "Yuh ain' no mo' 'feared o' me 'an ef a
wuz a lame hopper-grass. But a been't, a tell
yuh !" with sudden fierceness, "a'm a man, an' a
strong man, an' a loves yuh !"

He caught her to him, his face in a blaze, and
then gave a sharp bark of pain, as her teeth met
in the back of his hand.

"Damn yuh, furrer cole'-livered devil!" he cried,
shaking his bloody hand, and then, under a sudden
inspiration, flung himself upon the ground and
buried his face on his outstretched arm. Tanis
stood staring down at him. He had taken good
care that his wounded hand should be in full

view, and the girl's eyes fixed themselves, in horror, on the scarlet oval left by her strong teeth.

"A'm sorry," she muttered, after awhile, as he continued prone and motionless. "A'm sorry, Sam," she said again.

The blood, that continued to well over the back of his hand, made her faint. She stooped down, and, tearing off one of her apron-strings, began to bandage the wound. But he jerked away his hand, giving a smothered moan as he did so.

"Ain' yuh hyuh me seh a wuz sorry?" she asked, her voice trembling. "A did'n' mean tuh ack like a brute beas'. A 'clare, fo' Gawd, a did'n', but seems like yuh sots me crazy. A done know, harf th' time, whut a'm a-doin' when yuh 'gins tuh pester me."

Sam moaned again.

"Lemme wrop up yo' han'," she urged; "do, now, Sam. A 'ain' got no grudge 'gin yuh, 'cep'in' a knows yuh'se bad, an' a hain't a-goin' tuh keep comp'ny wi' no man ez is reel bad. A swar a hain't—a done keer ef hit kills me!"

Again he moaned, but this time consented to let her take his hand and wrap it up.

The western sun was dashing the floor of the forest with pools of amber and crimson. As she tied the last knot, she said, in an almost inaudible voice:

"A wisht yuh *wuz* a good feller, Sam."

"Why, honey?" he whispered.

"A dunno.   A wishes hit, though."

"Ud yuh keer fuh me ef a wuz gooder?"

"A dunno, but oh! a wishes yuh wuz."

"Look at me, honey.   Lawd, Lawd, what eyes!   Seems like a kin feel muhse'f a-sinkin' in 'em, like they wuz water.   Is muh eyes a-lookin' love at yuh, muh prutty?"

"A dunno—a cyarn't he'p lookin' at 'em, somehow." Her pupils began to dilate, and she breathed quickly.

"Yo eyes be the color o' cresses onder runnin' water," he said.   "What be the color o' mine?"

"Yo'n?" she asked, stammering.   "A—a dunno, a cyarn't see em good, a cyarn't.   Oh!"

She drew a long, shivering sigh. Their mouths seemed growing into one. She had never been kissed before, and, in spite of her protestations and honest avowals to the contrary, she loved him ; in spite of all the evil that she knew about him ; in spite of his wicked deeds, his cool cruelty, his calm, maddening vanity in regard to her feeling for him, she loved him. But when, at last, he threw back his head, and took the chill evening air deep into his nostrils, like a stag that has just drunk from a mountain stream, she started back, a look of shame and regret contorting all her face; then, without a word, turned and ran from him as swiftly as her nimble feet could carry her.

He did not attempt to follow, but leaned watching her, with the drowsy air of one half intoxicated. After awhile he lifted his bitten hand, and, pushing aside the bandage, fastened his lips on the marks of those vicious little teeth.

CHAPTER VII.

ABOUT nine o'clock that evening Tanis went to the window and looked out. From a sky of cold, black-blue, an icy moon was staring, blurred now and then by scudding wisps of cloud, and a low, rattling sound rose and fell in the bare apple orchard, for the wind was beginning to shake his frozen wings. A knot of snow-drops, near the door, looked as cold and bright as though cut out of silver.

Tanis unhooked a brown cloak which hung behind the kitchen door, and, throwing it about her, drew on a pair of leather mittens. The cloak had a loose hood, which she pulled over her head. Then, covering the bed of live coals on the hearth with ashes, she took her hickory staff in her hand, and, unlatching the door, stepped out into the waking gale.

About her were steep fields, showing a dull grayish green in the icy glare, rough with small stones and masses of lichen-covered rock.

The very sheep looked stonelike, as they lay, huddled in little knots, on the close-cropped turf. High above, on all sides, the sharp-toothed combs of the mountain striped the pale air as with steel. Their shadows slept beside the jagged boulders, like pools of frozen ink. The stunted oak trees, crowding about them, seemed to bristle as with iron ribs, and, as the girl looked upward, she fancied that the heavens resembled the roof of some vast cave, studded with starry icicles.

Her way led her next, for half a mile, along the highroad, and as she climbed the long slope known as "Cave Hill," she remembered the actual cave, on her right, in which a skeleton was said to have been found, and even gazed about her feverishly, for the tree on which a man was said to have hanged himself, after gambling away all that he possessed.

It thrust itself suddenly before her, like a contorted, gouty hand. She shuddered, in spite of predetermination, and swerved to the other side of the road; then, climbing the snake-fence opposite, struck out across the fields once more.

Now the wind, fully awake at last, rushed bellowing towards her, like a winged bull. With clenched teeth and body bent sturdily forward, she strove on faster than before, in spite of the strong beating of her cloak, which seemed trying to tug her backward. Again the blast struck her, this time from the side. She could hear the angry surging of the forest upon the mountain which she was nearing.

" T'on't be s'bad i' th' woods," she said aloud.

Her hood was stripped suddenly from her head, and her cloak, wrapping about her staff, almost jerked it from her grasp. But the sky was still as bright as ice, and the mad moon seemed racing past the flags of cloud.

Having reached the forest, she leaned against a tree for some moments, to regain her breath. All the ground was fluttering and rustling with last year's leaves. A horned owl gave forth its deep trombone note above her head. Another answered, far away.

Something stirred in the brush at her side, then darted suddenly past, and on down the steep declivity—a deer, with wide, moon-silvered antlers and swift, sure feet.

Tanis gave a cry of delight and leaped forward, all the huntress hot in her veins.

"Lawd, Lawd!" she groaned, "but that do make me mortal homesick. A cyarn't stan' hit much longer—a cyarn't. A wuz bawn i' th' mountains. We b'longs tuh each other. Seems like that thar house 'll kill me, sometimes. A wan't meant tuh live in a house, no more'n that deer wuz meant to wear a shell like a snail. Seems like a'd let hit all rip, jess tuh hev Bill an' a gun hyuh furrer minnit."

She gave a great sigh and began to walk on again.

Having skirted the side of the mountain, she came out into a narrow opening of level ground, through which a broad, stone-choked torrent crawled, glaring between its cress-grown banks. A cow lay under the tossing branches of a stunted apple tree, and, a few yards further on, she could

see a log cabin braced against an immense
boulder. Another sigh broke from her—this
time one of relief.

"Yease—thar hit be," she said, and began to
run toward it. For some moments she stood
knocking at the rickety door, before anyone answered. Then a voice called out, threateningly:

"Who be that a-poundin' thar, at this time o'
night?"

"A be Tanis, the sang-digger."

"An' what be yuh a-wantin', at this time o'
night, when only dead folks be a stirrin'?"

"A be a-wantin' yo' help, Aunt Libby. A wants
hit *bad*."

"Shore 'nuff! A'd swar tuh *that*. No human
wants *good*, at this time o' night. But ef yuh be
Tanis, the sang-digger, like yuh sez, let down yo'
har, an' I'll peek thoo' th' winder an' see whe'rr
yuh be a-lyin' or no."

The girl tore her heavy plait apart, with eager
fingers, and, standing before the window, shook
it about her, until she seemed wrapped in a fiery
veil.

"Yuh be she, shore's death!" piped the queru-
lous voice, and the next moment the door was
opened.

The figure that appeared in its fire-lit square
was small, twisted, unhuman-looking. Its coarse
white hair, whipped about by the fierce wind,
sprang from a forehead as brown and shriveled
as a dried tobacco-leaf. The eyes were two
glittering points. The huge nose overarched a
toothless cavity, and underneath it hung a goitre
in which the chin had been absorbed. But although so small and misshapen, the old woman
had the square, sturdy figure of a man, and
gorilla-like arms, reaching below her knees.

"Yuh be she, shore's hell!" she repeated.
"But huccum yuh hyuh, this time o' night?
Th' sang been't ready fur diggin'. An' whar be
yo' gang?"

"A'm cole, Aun' Libby," said the girl. "A've
walked a long way, an' a'm frez tuh th' bone.
Lemme in tuh warm, an' a'll tell yuh all yuh ax."

But the woman stretched out one of her long
arms, barring the way.

"How be a tuh know ef yuh be alone?" she asked, suspiciously. "How be a tuh know yo' gang hain' a-waitin' i' th' bresh, tuh murder me bime-by?"

Tanis made a curious sign with both hands, and then said:

"A swar by th' tokin a'm alone."

"Then come in an' warm," said the hag.

The girl followed her into a low, smoke-blackened room, in one end of which a wide fireplace was glowing, fed by great logs or rather trees, for the trunks of two chestnut saplings lay along the pine floor, their withered leaves still clinging to the smaller branches, which had not been cut away, their crowns snapping and crackling among the chunks of "fat-wood" on the hearth.

There was no bedstead. A heap of rags filled one corner of the room, covered by a filthy log-cabin quilt. Upon this lay two pillows, made of old trouser-legs, filled with shucks and twisted up at each end by a bit of string. Upon one of these rested a shaggy mat of black hair and beard.

Its owner was snoring heavily.

"A wanted tuh speak tuh yuh by yo'se'f, Aun' Libby," whispered Tanis, her face falling.

"Well, a be by muhse'f," said the other, grinning, if a toothless gaping of leathern lips can be called a grin. "Dave's drunk, an' a drunk man hain't man nor 'ooman, nor ghose, nor nuthin'. So talk away, muh prutty."

Tanis sat down on a three-legged pine stool, black with use and grease, while the old woman drew up the one cane-bottomed chair, quite as greasy, if not as black, and taking down her clay pipe from one of the projecting stones of the chimney, began to fill it, her keen eyes searching the girl's troubled face as she did so. Here and there, on other stones, stood bottles of different sizes and colors, earthenware jugs, battered tin cans, gourds and bags of coarse, dirty stuff, tied up by bits of rag. From a rope which hung between two nails, just within reach, dangled bunches of herbs, roots, and curiously shaped seed-pods. A table in one corner held two broken plates, a blue and white china cup, and a little, round looking-glass, in a frame made from pine cones. In the opposite corner stood two guns.

When she had lighted her pipe to her satisfaction, the old witch spoke again:

"Be yo' arrand too bad fuh wuds?" she asked slowly.

Tanis started. Her face was white and grim. She returned the other's gaze boldly.

"Naw. A hain't nuvver ben on a arrand yet as a wuz 'shamed tuh tell 'bout," she answered, "an' a hain't a-goin' tuh begin now."

"Well, talk then," said the woman.

"A reckon folks come tuh yuh fuh prutty much ev'y thing onder th' sun—done they, Aun' Libby?"

"Prutty much."

"Fuh love-drinks an' sech truck mos' ev'y day, a reckon. Hein?"

"Ev'y day, an' ev'y night, mos'." She took out her pipe, and hunching her shoulders, leered comfortably at the beautiful face opposite.

"Be hit love ez hev caught yun at larst, honey?"

"That hain' nuther hyuh nor thar," said Tanis,

sternly. "But a hain't come tuh yuh fuh no love-truck, Aun' Libby."

A faint gleam of surprise smouldered, for a moment, in the peering eyes.

"Yuh hain't come furrer love-drink? Well, an' fuh whut then, Tanis Gribble?"

The girl answered the question by another, suddenly put. She leaned forward so that she could see the horrible old face more clearly.

"Aun' Libby," she said, "yuh wuz a gal onct like me. A've heerd folks say ez how yuh wuz mortal prutty, too."

The hag stared for a moment, and then actually bridled.

"Them want no liars, nuther, ez tole yuh that," she observed, blandly. "Yuh see these hyuh eyes? They hain't no bigger'n partridge berries, now, an' they be mos' ez red, but when a war a gal, they want no blue bird ez war bluer. They want no glarss button ez war brighter. An' this hyuh skin er mine—" she picked up a fold from her wrinkled arm and held it, while gazing upon it with deep contempt, "this hyuh skin er mine, whut's ez loose

an' brown ez a dawg's hide now, they want no
whitewash ez war whiter.   When a hed cheeks,
too, they wuz pinker'n a cirkis gal's legs, en muh
har was ez long ez yo'n, an' a darn sight pruttier
color.   T'war yaller ez broom straw, 'n' hed a skin
on hit like a new bottle, an' muh toofs mought a
ben chipped outerrer chiny plate."

She stuck her pipe back between the gums once
ornamented by those very teeth, and drew several
quick puffs.   "Yease, a war prutty onct," she said,
decisively.

"An' war yuh ever in love, Aun' Libby?"

There was silence for a few moments; then the
woman answered slowly :

"Hit like turrer bu'nt me up, same's fire bu'ns
up a house."

Tanis drew her stool a little nearer.

"Tell me 'bout hit—tell me!" she urged
eagerly.   "Wuz he prutty, too?   Wuz he big
'n' strong?   Did he hev blue eyes, like yo'n?—an'
teeth like chiny?   An' war he good or bad?   War
he good tuh wimmins, or did he fool wi' 'em?   Did
he act squar by yuh, or did he fool yuh?"

The hag took out her pipe and again gaped mirthfully upon the girl.

"Do a *look* like a'd ben fooled much, honey?"

"Naw, yuh pintly don't," said Tanis, bluntly.

"An' a pintly wa'n't! But, namergawd, hit wrinched me!"

Tanis was all eagerness, in a flash.

"Did hit go suh hard wi' yuh, Aun' Libby? Did hit now? Did yuh hev tormint? War he bad? Did'n' he love yuh?"

"Love me nuthin', yuh little fool! Men done *love*, they *wants*, an' when they *gits*, they done want no mo'!"

"But did yuh marh'y him?"

The woman cackled harshly.

"A war a sang-digger, same's yuh, muh prutty!" she said. "An' thar's one thing whar sang-diggers is like heaven. Thar hain' no mar'hyn nor givin' in mar'hidge wi' um! Hee! hee! But a tuk Joe fuh muh man, ef that's what yuh wants tuh git at."

The girl's face had grown scarlet, but she said steadily:

" An' war he good tuh yuh ?"

"A hed nine chil'n by him, an' he beat 'em mo'n he beat me. That war supp'n. But he got on a drunk an' kilt ma pap, an' *that* war sup'n, too. Then a lef' 'im."

"Oh, he wuz bad, then! he wuz bad, too!" cried the girl, with a sob. She let her head drop forward in her hands, but the same instant the old woman clutched her by the shoulder, shaking her fiercely.

"Gawdamoughty! Hyuh! Shet yo' mouf! Done yuh jaw my Joe or hit'll be wuss fuh yuh !"

She looked like a fiend, her little eyes blazing, her shapeless face working with rage. Both hands were grasping the girl's shoulders now. Her pipe lay broken on the stone hearth.

"Shet yo' cussed mouf! Shet it, a say !" she cried, shrilly. "Hit alluz did sot me mad tuh hyuh a bad wud agin Joe! Namergawd, done yuh seh no mo'! A dunno what a'll do tuh yuh ! T'ain' safe ! T'ain' safe !"

But Tanis did not know what fear meant. She said quietly:

"Thar now, sober down, Aun' Libby. A cert'n'y hain't meant tuh hut yo' feelin's. Of cose I dunno nothin' bout hit." She stooped and picked up the broken pipe. "Ken a git yurrer 'nother?" she asked.

But Aunt Libby had sunk back into her chair, shaking and speechless. Her eyes glared before her, as though looking at some one invisible to Tanis.

"Muh po' ole Joe! Muh po' ole man!" the girl heard her muttering. "No one hain' nuvver done yuh jestice savin' me."

After a while she got up, still trembling, and filled herself another pipe. When she had smoked for ten minutes in silence, she turned to the girl as though nothing had happened.

"Well, an' what be yuh a-wantin'?"

"What be a a-wantin'?" repeated Tanis, slowly. "Well, a'll tell yuh. A wants supp'n ez'll kill love in man an' 'ooman both. Supp'n ez 'll kill hit dead ez Adam 'fore he wuz made."

The expression of Aunt Libby was indescribable.

"Supp'n - ez—'ll—*kill*—love?" she repeated.
"Supp'n—ez—'ll—kill—*love?*" She sat, open-
mouthed, blinking up at Tanis, who was now
standing to her full height above her, pale again,
and determined.

"Yease, supp'n ez 'll kill love. Supp'n ez 'll
kill hit so hit 'on't hev even a *ghose.* Thet's what
a wants, Aun' Libby."

"Supp'n ez'll kill *love!* Supp'n ez'll kill *love!*"
droned the witch, still gaping at her. Then, with
a sudden flash, as from a fire smouldered to its
last coal: "Yuh fool! Yuh hain't got th' sence
yuh wuz bawned wi'! Done yuh know ez how
po' folks hain't got but *two* pleasures i' th' whole
worl', yuh fool! Look at Dave thar! They hain'
no king nor rich man alive ez is got mo'n Dave's
got, now he's full o' whisky! Talk o' Heaven!
When a body's full o' whisky heaven's *in* em!
They done need tuh sot out tuh *fine* hit.
'Ud hit take mo' whisky tuh mek th' man
ez owns the Hot Springs drunker'n Dave be
now? An' ud he be happier? When yuh're
drunk yuh're drunk—an' when yuh're drunk

yuh're happy—'n' happiness is but happiness.
An' when yuh love hit's th' same. Cud a queen
love more'n you cud? 'N' cud th' man ez she
loved, an' ez loved her, mek a queen happier'n yo'
man cud mek you? *Fool!* Love an' whisky's
all us po' folks is got tuh pay us fuh th' cussedness uv life. 'N' then them ez is rich pints at us
an' calls us *low!* Books 'n' theayters, 'n' fine close,
'n' hawses, 'n' ridin' on th' cyars, 'n' sailin' tuh
strange contris—*they* kin git fat 'n' good 'n' happy
on sech things, an' go tuh heaven arterwards, too!
But sang-diggers an' th' like! Wut is *we* got?
Wut is th' like uv yuh'n me 'n' Dave yonder got
tuh switch up our blood 'n' make us better'n
sticks 'n' stones 'n' graveyard worms? Love 'n'
whisky! Love 'n' whisky, yuh fool! When
yuh're young like *you* be—love; 'n' when yuh're
ole, like *I* be—whisky."

She fell back, panting, and the girl stood as
though transfixed, gazing at her from wide, horri-
fied eyes. At last she said, almost in a whisper:

"Fuh Gawd's sake, Aun' Libby, gimme what a
axed yuh fuh an' lemme go! A done mean a

wants yuh tuh kill *all* th' love in me, but a wants
to stop lovin' one man. An' a wants him tuh stop
lovin' me. He's bad. He's bad, thoo' and thoo',
an' a wants hit tuh end now. A've stood 'nuff.
Hit's like hell-fire in muh heart."

She had clasped her hands together as she spoke,
and now held them out to the other, beseechingly.

"Oh, Aun' Libby ! A'll do mos' *anythin'* fuh
yuh ef yuh'll gimme supp'n tuh kill jess this hyuh
one love, 'caze hit's a bad love. Hit'll mek me bad,
'n' hit'll brek Bill's heart, 'n' hit'll do harm tuh
others ! Aun' Libby, a hain' nuvver prayed in
muh life, but oh ! ef yuh'll gimme a drink ez'll do
that, a'll pray ev'ry night on muh bended knees
fuh Gawd tuh give yuh back yo' Joe one day
somewhar, an' let *him* be like he war when yuh
loved him, 'n' let *you* be yorng 'n' pretty like yuh
war when he loved you !"

She was too blinded by her own tears to see the
meagre drops that had oozed from the other's
parched lids and crept over the withered cheeks
as she was speaking ; but, as she finished, the poor
old wretch rose trembling from her chair, and

again put both crooked hands upon the young shoulders, now shaken with sobs.

"Honey," she whispered, faintly, then pausing and trying to steady her voice.

"Done cry, honey! A'll do th' bes' a ken fuh yuh. A've got a drink. T'one hut yuh. But—but—mebbe——" She paused again and looked about her, vaguely. "Mebby," she ended, "yuh'd better seh yo' prars 'bout that thar, too."

When Tanis turned to leave the cabin the moon was just slipping over the crest of Back-creek mountain and the wind had lulled.

As she put the vial which Aunt Libby had given her in the breast of her gown, she turned, under a sudden impulse, and, stooping, pressed her fresh lips to that seamed forehead.

The old wretch clung to her for a moment, and the girl fancied that she heard her sob.

CHAPTER VIII.

THE weather had changed suddenly. The pale spring sky had drooped low over the valley like a soft, perfumed, breeze-stirred veil. The lilacs were beginning to distil their honeyed scent, and the clustering water-cresses were sprinkled with little bright yellow blossoms, whose reflections streaked the water running past them as with wavy perpendicular sunbeams. There was a stir of young life throughout the deep forests and in the grass of the fields.

Tanis sat with her elbows on the side of the kitchen window, her chin in her palms, her eyes trying to make out the curves and angles of some constellations which Alice had shown her the night before. But her face had an absent-minded expression. Evidently the stars touched only the surface of her mood.

She withdrew her eyes from their bright mazes after some moments, and fixing them on the dusky mountain side, only a few yards away, said aloud, but in a low, concentrated voice :

"Come tuh me! Come tuh me! A needs yuh! A *mus'* see yuh."

The silky rustle of the night wind, blowing fitfully, brought with it the sound of a warm brooklet that trilled through the field below, its course marked by delicate whorls of steam, while a nestful of unfledged birds, in the quince tree near by, set up sleepy twitterings as their cradle bough swayed gently.

"Come tuh me!" said the girl again, her brows knit in her intensity, her hands grasped together. "Ef yuh ken feel me a-callin' tuh yuh, Come! *Come!*"

Shortly a new sound caught her ear, the sound of a man's step—long, impatient. She rose at once, unlatching the door, and, opening it wide, stood waiting upon the threshold.

A tall figure soon came in sight and moved rapidly up the garden path.

"S'that you, Sam?" she asked, in quiet tones.

"That's me, honey," came the quick response.

He approached and was about to take her in his
arms, when she drew back, putting out one hand
to keep him from her.

"Ef yuh loves me like yuh says, yuh'll come in
an' ack like a tells yuh," she then remarked. "A
wants tuh hev a good talk wi' yuh, Sam Rose. A
wants yuh tuh 'have yuhse'f same ez ef Bill wuz
hyuh, an' a wants yuh tuh hyuh me thoo' wi'
what a got tuh seh."

He tried to make out the expression of her face
in the starlight, but failed.

"Well," he answered, almost meekly. "G'long.
A'll foller."

When they were both in the kitchen, Tanis lifted
the glaring kerosene lamp from the shelf beside
the window and set it on the long deal table between them, then signed him to place two chairs.
He put them close together, but she removed them
at once a full yard apart. Sam grinned and looked
puzzled. He had stuck a spray of dark blue wild
flowers in his hat, and their color brought out the
downright gold of his beard and accentuated the
azure of his eyes. He leaned back, quite conscious

of his own charms, and slowly caressed his beard, the strong fibres drawing down his under lip at each movement and disclosing its clear scarlet.

"Well, muh prutty," he said, still smiling at her, "an' what be th' tex' uv yo' sarmon?"

Tanis looked at him very gravely.

"'Tain't no sarmon," she said. "An', fust uv all, a wants yuh tuh tell me huccum yuh hyuh tuh night?"

"A come 'caze a felt yuh a-drawin' uv me, beauty bright."

She grew very pale.

"S'that hones'?" she asked, in a low voice.

"'That's hones'," he replied, nodding easily.

"A wonders, a wonders—" she began, and then broke off and stared at him with troubled speculation in her eyes.

"Yuh wonders what, sugar?" he urged, and slipped his chair a little nearer to hers by an almost imperceptible movement. "What is hit yuh wonders? Tell Sam. He b'longs tuh yuh, same ez yo' own han' or fut or heart do. C'yarn't yuh tell him?"

"Mebbe," she said, shortly. And then, rising, "but fust a'm a-goin' tuh let Mis' Gilman know you'se hyuh. A hain't nuvver done nothin' on th' sly, an' a hain't a-goin' tuh begin now."

He stared at her, actually speechless, and before he had recovered from his surprise she had left the room.

As usual, Alice was lying on her sofa with a book. She put it down when Tanis entered, and smiled at her. But the girl was too troubled to smile back. She came close to the pretty sofa, with its coverlet of silk and lace, and said bluntly:

"A come tuh tell yuh ez how a feller, called Sam Rose, be i' th' kitchen. He be a sang-digger an' a bad 'un, but he says ez how he loves me, an' mebbe a ken talk him into some goodness." She caught her breath and then went on: "A—a loves him, too—but 'tain't a good love, hit done do me no good. A wanter try tuh mek hit wuk on him good, though, an'—an' then, mebbe, we mought come together some day an' be happy." She paused again; then with shyness and great stumbling over her words: "A hain't nuvver hed much

call tuh pray. Hit done come natchul tuh me, but
you be so good—'ud yuh mine—'ud hit worrit
yuh, tuh—tuh say a good wud tuh Gawd fuh Sam
'n' me? A come tuh tell yuh he war hyuh, cazė
a mought be a argyfyin' wi' him twel right late,
he's that mulish, an' a wanted yuh tuh know
't'warn' fuh no harm a wuz a-keepin' uv him."

Alice drew her down and kissed her, in silence,
but the girl understood this simple act better
than she would have done the most eloquent
phrases.

When she entered the kitchen again Sam had
found some corn bread and honey in a cupboard
and was regaling himself freely, whistling between
his immense bites and cutting pigeon-wings over
the blackened floor. He stuffed the last morsel
into his mouth as she appeared, and made a lunge
at her with both arms, but she slipped past him
and seated herself at the table. He laughed good-
naturedly, and took the chair which he had placed
for himself at her request.

"Now," he said, wiping on his trouser leg the
big clasp-knife with which he had been hacking

his corn-pone and honey. "Fire away. All' stan' stiddy, fuh a targit."

There was silence for some moments, broken by the rusty ticking of the old mahogany clock on the chimney-piece, and the intermittent *frou-frou* of the breeze in a stack of fodder near the open window.

Then, lifting her grave eyes to his, the girl said slowly:

"*How* duz yuh love me, Sam?"

He looked staggered for a moment, and then that ever-ready smile shortened his face and narrowed his keen eyes.

"*How* duz a *love* yuh?" he repeated. "My lawdy, sugar, but thet's th' dawggones' thing uvver a hyearn! A love yuh, same ez other fellers loves a gal, when they wants her wuss'n whisky."

Tanis winced. Those words "want" and "whisky" brought Aunt Libby before her like an actual presence.

"Yease, *thet's* hit," she returned, dryly. "Mebbe *you* calls *wantin'* jess so, *lovin'*, but *I* don't."

Sam shook his shoulders, impatiently.

"When a man loves a gal, done he alluz want her?" he demanded.

"Yease, but thar's moughty diff'unt ways o' wantin'. Some wants a bird tuh *eat* hit, an' some wants hit tuh take keer uv hit an' larn hit how tuh sing. What *I* wants tuh know is this hyuh—how long'd yuh love me, arter yuh got me?"

"Now, honey," said Sam, looking serious for the first time, "ef any man lays out tuh tell a gal percizely *how long* he's a-goin' tuh love her, that man's a darned liar, or, if he ain't, then he's a darned fool. A ken tell yuh one thing, tho'. A loves you wuss'n a uvver loved a gal sence a wuz bawn. Hit fyar gneaws me like honger an' thust. Seems like sometimes, ef a cuddn't ketch a holt o' yuh, a'd lie down an' die. Ef a wus starvin' en a hed muh chice 'twixt a bite o' bread an' yo' mouf, a'd kiss yuh an' quit."

She was flushed and trembling, but very quiet.

"That been't *all*, though, be it?" she asked. "Dontchu nuvver feels like yuh'd want tuh be a better man, fur my sake? Dontchu nuvver feels like you wanted tuh be good, fuh me?"

"A feel like a'd like tuh be good *tuh you*, muh prutty. A done know ez how a hones arter bein' suh good *fuh* yuh. What i' th' namersense hez goodness gotter do wi' lovin'? A reckons the Ole Scratch hisse'f loves his 'ooman, an' *he* cyarn't mix up much *goodness* wi' hit."

Her face was white and anxious.

"But, Sam, arter we got mah'd, s'pos'n' then yuh stopped a-lovin' me like yuh duz now, 'ud yuh go on wi'—wi' yo' badness to'ds other gals? Ud yuh alluz swar, an' drink, an' shoot, like yuh ben do all yuh life? Oh, Sam, 'tain't suh much good rightaway ez a 'spects yuh tuh be, but tuh *want* tuh, *want* tuh, be gud."

Sam gazed at her soberly.

"Gawd, *He* knows yuh beats me!" he said at last, "but a sut'n'y hain't a-goin' tuh lie fuh nobordy." One of his sudden inspirations seized him. "Hyuh!" he said, patting his knee, "come hyuh, an' set on muh lap, an' a'll try tuh mek *my* way o' thinkin' cl'ar to you."

At first she hesitated, but something in his

eyes compelled her, and she went reluctantly toward him. He lifted her on his knee, then, folding both arms about her, pressed her closer and closer to him, until her breath came painfully.

"'Thar! *that's* how a loves yuh," he exclaimed at last. "Now kiss me, an' a'll show yuh plainer yit."

But she tore herself away.

"Yuh're *bad*, an' yuh wants tuh *stay* bad," she cried, passionately ; "how *kin* the Lawd be gud, like folks say, and yit mek mens like you ?"

"Ef yuh loved me, yuh wouldn't bother me wi' all this hyuh truck o' talk", he said, doggedly, as pale as she was, "but you mought ez well be made outer tin fuh all *you* kin feel. Yuh dunno what love is. Mebbe yuh"ll know, some day, an' mebbe yuh wone wanter wase s'much time a-talkin', but by Gawdamoughty, a'll kill th' feller ez yuh loves, ef he be a angel dude fresh from heaven."

The girl's eyes flashed.

"How *dar*' yuh seh what a feels an what a done feel?" she cried. "How *dar*' yuh tell me whe'rr a loves yuh or no? Ain't *I* got a heart, an' a brain, an' a bordy same as *you* is? Ain't *I* got blood i' muh veins, an' tears back o' muh eyes, same ez any other gal? 'Case a done want tuh tek up wi' a drunkard an' a gambler, an' a feller what goes 'bout doin' wus'n murder, yuh dar' stan' thar an' tell me a done feel!"

Her mood broke suddenly, and left her radiant with tears.

"Oh, Sam, Sam!" she pleaded, "done tormint me no mo'. A is been love yuh sence a fust seed yuh, tell hit seemed like muh vurry har bu'nt me a-blowin' roun' muh face. A is ben honger arter yuh, tell hit seemed like thar warn' no place on earth ez empty ez these hyuh arms o' mine. A is ben thurst tuh look inter yuh eyes, twel hit seemed like mine wuz dryin' up wi' fever. When yuh kissed me, that day, on th' Warm Springs mountain, hit seemed like a wuz meltin' away in yo' arms—like a wuz you, yo'se'f—like a breathed wi' yo' breath an' looked wi' yo' eyes. When a thinks how tall yuh is muh heart jumps i' muh bres' like a hot stone. When a 'members yuh voice, an' th' sweet wuds yuh done seh tuh me, hit seems like a wuz faintin' back inter a dream. Sometimes, i' th' dark, a've thunk ez how yuh kissed me, an' it seemed like sparks o' fire was pourin' over me, an' thoo me, same ez they does up th' chimbly when yuh beats on smoulderin' wood. *Thet's* how a loves yuh, Sam, but oh, a loves yuh more'n *thet*. A loves yuh so, a'd gi' muh life tuh see yuh jess *a-wantin'* tuh be good. When a sez good, a done mean like them whinin' preachers i' th' valley, but kynd an' hones' wi' gals, not suh often drunk, not suh quick tuh cut an' shoot an' drag others inter sin."

She paused, gasping, her hands clasped against her breast, her eager eyes thrust deep into his.

His face was flushed with conflicting passions. He opened and shut his great hands nervously in his effort to control himself. He was angry, touched, resentful, while over all his love for her swelled with a mad rage.

"How be yuh a-goin' tuh *prove* all this hyuh moughty *love* o' yourn?" he said, at last, in a thick voice. "How be yuh a-goin' tuh mek me b'lieye yuh hongers arter me, when yuh 'on't even gi' me a kiss? Ef yuh suh moughty hongry arter suppin', 'udn't yuh tek a bite o' hit? Naw, by Gawd, ef yuh loved me like yuh seh yuh do, thar 'udn't be no room in yuh fuh *reason.* Yo' arms 'ud be wropped roun' muh neck same ez ef yuh wuz drowndin', an' yuh mouf 'ud be fars tuh mine, like yuh wuz drawin' yuh vurry life outer me. *Love!* *you* love! yuh dunno no mo' 'bout love 'n' ef yuh hed'n ben weaned but yestiddy! Why, ez yuh stans thar a-gapin' at me, them red lips o' yourn wars th' shape o' yo' mammy's bres' yit!" He actually groaned, "Lawd! Lawd! yuh po' little baby-gal! 'Ooman folks done stan' in arm's-reach o' th' fellers they loves, an' jaw 'bout th' *right* an' *wrong* uv it, ez ef they war in Sunday-school, an' ez cool an' green ez cowcumbers. A reckons one o'

them critters ez lives at the north pole an' chaws
on taller candles tuh keep 'em warm, a reckons one
o' them coots ud suit yuh fustrate. They'd love
yuh th' way yuh'd like to be loved, a reckon.
Somebordy tole me ez how they *rubbed noses* 'sted o'
kissin'!" He laughed savagely. "Yease, *them'd*
be 'bout th' kine *you'd* like tuh manage. By thun-
der! yuh *hev'* got cole grit tuh drag in goodness, by
th' yers a-squealin' like a pig, an' thin go a-tell'n'
me ez hit an' love's got tuh be mixed 'fore yuh'll
tase hit!" He took a stride forward, but did not
attempt to touch her. "You're a gal, an' mebbe
all this sort o' truck done wuk yuh up, like hit do
a man. Mebbe *you* kin stan' thar an' preach at
me an' *enjie* yuhse'f, but I hain't no gal! I hain't
no mealy-moufed Mithydis, an' th' blood's a-bub-
blin' in me same's melted iron! D'yuh think a'm
a-going on furuvver, a-lettin' yuh make a cawn-
geygashun out o' me, an' a twis'n' up them prutty
lips o' yourn wi' Bible wuds an' sich, when muh
vurry heart's a-whirlin' in me, a wants tuh kiss yuh
so? D'yuh think *that?* 'Caze ef yer does, by th'
whole crowd o' Heaven, yuh thinks a lie. Thar'll

come a time when a wone stan' hit no mo', an' then
yuh'll wisht yuh heddn't druv me crazy ! "

Tanis stood gazing fearlessly upon him, magnifi-
cent and white.

" *Yease*," she said, as he paused, out of breath.
" *Yease*, thet thar's th' way men talks tuh wimmen
ez tries tuh keep decent, an' do whut's right, so far
ez they knows how. Pore blind mole ! Cyarn't
yuh see no further'n yo' own craziness ? Cyarn't
yuh tell th' diff' ence t'wix' a 'ooman ez is bawn
cole an' puny, an' a 'ooman ez is wile an' strong by
nature, an' is tryin' tuh love i' th' bes' way ? Oh,
shame on yuh, shame! shame! tuh seh sich wuds tuh
me, when a've split open muh vurry heart fur yuh
tuh look at, when a've tole you how a've ached tuh
kiss yuh, an' a didn' do hit, jess caze 't'ud a ben
wrong! Yuh sehs I done know what love is! Well, a
say th' same tuh yuh! Yuh done love *me*, Sam Rose !
you loves th' *kisses* muh mouf cud give yuh, you
loves the *feel* muh arms 'ud hev on yuh th'oat, yuh
loves th' warmness ez 'ud go thoo' yuh ef a let
yuh hole me close, like yuh did jess now ! But
ain' that th' way yuh loves whisky ? Ain't hit fuh

th' *feel* hit gives yuh that yuh loves hit? 'Tain't th' stuff hitse'f no mor'n hit's me, muhse'f, yuh loves. Y'ud hut me, fuh yo' pleasure, quick ez thinkin', yuh'd make Bill hate me, an' yud leave me tuh muh mis'ry arterwards, like you lef' them po' Darley gals—an'—*Maggie*."

His face had grown so ghastly that she paused, half-awed by her own daring.

He sank into one of the chairs by the deal table. He was trembling. In one leap she had reached his side. Kneeling, she took his hand in both her own and pressed it against her heart.

"Sam, Sam," she stammered, "ef thar be a Gawd, *He* knows a'm a sayin' hit fuh yo' own sake. *He* knows a loves yuh, ev'n ef *you* don't. Fuhgive me—ef a've hit yuh too hard, an' try, try tuh feel th' love ez is back uv hit all."

He tried to speak, but his lips were dry. Fetching a gourd of water, she held it to his mouth with shaking hands. He drank eagerly, like a man in a fever, then said, huskily:

"Thar hain't nawbordy knows how—how—that gal hev harnted me night 'n' day."

"Oh, Sam! Oh, my dear Sam! Hev she? Be yuh sorry yuh done hit? Be yuh weak when yuh thinks uv hit? Do hit come tuh yuh by night an mek yuh fret an' tun 'bout in yo' bed?"

"Hit do! Hit do! Jess like yuh're a-sayin', Tanis. Them other gals wuz bold 'n' for'ard; a man ud a ben a fool tuh spar 'em. But th' other— she war a pitiful little critter. She sot a heap by me. A done her a devil's turn, Tanis." He got to his feet. "Thar, a reckons yuh'd better lemme go while muh blood's tunned tuh water, like it be now. Yuh're right, muh gal, a'm a low-down, bad feller, an' not fit tuh call yo' name—but—but——" He stared down at her, a little of the old fierceness lighting his eyes.

"Done you tarnt me no mo' wi' not lovin' yuh! Hit's like a said, devils ken love, a reckon. An' a feller tole me onct 'twar i' th' Bible ez how a devil loved a 'ooman. Thet's how a loves yuh, a reckon, an' hit's moughty strong—stronger'n I be, by a darn sight! But ef a ken keep a right rank kyerb 'twix' hit's jaws, a'll try to fool hit inter thinkin' a'm th' master, same ez folkses fools a hawse. Ef a ken hole out a won't pester yuh no mo'. Mine tho', a seh *ef a ken hole out !*"

He took up his hat from the table and was starting towards the door, when she stopped him. She came and slipped her hand shyly but firmly under his arm. A lovely smile lighted her face.

"Sam," she whispered, "come along o' me. A've got suppin' tuh show yuh."

The great fellow, dumb with surprise, allowed himself to be led around the side of the house, up to one of the front windows. The chintz curtains inside did not quite meet, and they could see the charming room beyond, with its glow of lamp and firelight, its bowls of daffodils and gleaming books and pictures.

On a crimson divan near the fire lay Alice, her blonde hair unfastened and falling about her face. Gilman was seated in a low chair beside her, a book in one hand, the other resting between his wife's fragile palms. He was reading to her, but every now and then they looked at each other and smiled. Sometimes she would put up one of her hands to his lips, with a winning gesture, and he

would kiss it softly between each word. Sometimes it was his hand that she touched to her
cheek. Once he got up to put some wood on the
fire, which was kept burning, although it was so
warm without, and as he came back he bent over
and gathered her slight figure to his breast, where
she clung happily, her fingers in his dark curls.
Once he kissed her, a slow, tender kiss, upon the
lips, and insisted upon drawing the coverlet higher
about her shoulders, although she protested that
she was not cold. Then, again, he began to read
to her. They could not hear the words, but from
the rhythmic beat of his voice they guessed that
it was " varses " of some kind.

" Come on—come away," whispered Tanis, suddenly, as though waking. " 'Tain't right tuh listen
tuh 'em. Come away, Sam."

So intense had been their absorption into those
other lives that she was as unconscious of Sam's
arm about her, as he had been of putting it there;
but now as she turned to speak to him, she felt
that she was in his embrace. This time, however,
she made no effort to escape.

"Dear Sam," she said, still under her breath, "that's what *I* calls love. Oh, a would love tuh be loved like that!"

He was still very gentle and awed, but he could not repress a smile at these words.

"Lawd! honey," he whispered back, "you mought ez well look furrer a whisky bottle tuh run milk! A hain't that kynd, an'"—he paused and looked at her a little mischievously in the dawning moonlight—"a done reckon *you* favors thet thar 'ooman nuther, ez much ez yuh mought. Yuh hain't th' kynd men loves like that, muh prutty."

"But, Sam, 'udn't a leetle o' that mixed in wi' th' other make hit all th' better?"

Sam shook his head rather dubiously.

"Dunno," he said, honestly. "A alluz did like muh whisky straight."

"But we 'ooman folks, Sam, we likes a dash o' milk or water in ourn. An' look at a mint julep, Sam! Thet's got sugar an' mint an' water, too, in hit, an' yuh fellers cert'n'y does love a good julep. Oh!"—she broke off suddenly, resting her clasped hands against his breast—" ef yuh only 'ud want tuh be gooder, Sam! ah'd let muhse'f go then! A'd love yuh mo'n a gal uvver loved a man befo', since th' worl' began."

CHAPTER IX.

A WEEK had passed. Again Tanis leaned at the open kitchen window. Behind her, in the shadow, was a gleam of copper and brass and newly-polished tin. The white muslin curtains made a film about her glowing face. She was like a pink peony wreathed in morning mist. In the black mould underneath the window, purple crocuses were springing, with here and there a golden one, to intensify their royalty. The apple trees were fairy tents of blossom. The peach tree branches swayed and hummed with clinging bees. Beyond, the mountains rose like pyramids of delicate marble, mottled with divers greens, and the faint crimson of the red-bud. Sky and earth seemed blowing gently in the soft, voluminous wind. It sent waves of perfume from myriad wild flowers rippling down the valley, over the warm brooklets, across the stern rampart of the hills. The clouds seemed to curl into airy folds beneath it, the forests swayed tenderly, and the

song of birds trembled, now low, now loud, as the
eddying gusts bore them forward or backward.

It was like an Easter-tide of nature. "Spring
is risen—is risen, and summer is binding on her
golden sandals. Spring is risen," murmured the
mountain streams; "winter is in the grave, and
no more will his beard of icicles choke our
sources and frighten our flags from blossoming."

The sun, parting the gay curtain of his bed,
looked lovingly upon the love-sick earth. The
oaks were hale and young again with rising sap.
Again the dog-wood felt an ecstasy of bloom and
whitened the water with virginal reflections. On
the stag's broad front the antlers were downy, as
with moss, and pliant like young willow twigs.
The eyes of the doe were bright and liquid, and
her flanks softer than velvet. Children's voices
sounded gaily through the valley. The ewes
were bleating in answer to the new-born lambs.
Through the warm, sweet-scented air the pollen
floated like specks of musty gold.

Tanis dreamed open-eyed at the window, and
all her dreams were of love. "Ef he war only

good," she thought. "Ef he only wanted tuh be good, how I cud love him! How I cud make him love me back! Ef hit war only right, and he hones' an' meanin' well by me, how I cud rest in his arms, an' give him back his kisses! How sweet it 'ud be, to kiss him an' know hit 'twant a sin! His eyes be bluer'n them little flowers thar! I'd kiss 'em twel they shut, same as th' flowers do, when a bee tickles 'em. I cud make him trimble, same ez them peach boughs trimble i' th' wind, though he do be suh strong an' tall! He thinks a don' keer—that a'm cole an' proud—that his kisses worrits me! Oh, how s'prised he'd be ef a lem' muhse'f go an' loved him, like a yearns tuh. Oh, Sam, Sam! muh own man, ef you only *wanted* tuh be good!"

It was at this moment that Sam opened the garden gate and walked towards her. His flannel shirt was clean, and disclosed fully the splendid modelling of chest and arms. His blue eyes seemed to partake of the universal joyousness about them. He walked fast and vigorously, so that a few strides brought him close to Tanis.

"Honey," he asked in a triumphant whisper, "whatchu think? A ain't teched a drap o' whisky sence a lars' saw yuh!"

"Ain't yuh, Sam?"

She looked more like a peony than ever. The little white kerchief knotted about her throat reminded him of a snow-wreath on a flower. He could see her thin, pink cotton gown beat with her quick breathing.

"A'm a tryin' tuh do whut yuh wants, Tanis," he went on. Then he ventured to smooth back a stray lock and tuck it behind one of her warm, downy ears.

"A'm a-tryin' tuh *wanter* want tuh be good."

"Air yuh?" she breathed, not daring to meet his eyes. "Air yuh, Sam? Hit cert'n'y is kynd o' yuh."

"But oh, darlin'," he hurried to add, "A cyarn't he'p thinkin' t'ould come so much quicker ef yud he'p me long wi' a bit o' love, now an' agin."

She took his great hand from her throat, and pressed it between both her own.

"A does love yuh, Sam, an' yuh knows hit."

"But tain't th' kynd o' love a wants," he urged, breathlessly. "A wants yuh tuh come tuh me, same ez a flame turrer a match when hit's struck, same ez a bee turrer apple tree. A wants yuh tuh git love-mad, same ez steers git water-mad, and bolt fuh me thro' ev'y thin' ez lies a-tween us. Oh! ma own gal, gi' me one kiss!"

He drew her, panting and troubled, to his breast. Their eyes darkened on each other, their breath was mingled, and then, with a sudden effort, she wrenched herself away, and stood paling and reddening, before him, her eyes on her intertwisted hands. He lounged on the window-sill, pulling at his beard, puzzled, disappointed, but not angry.

"Lawd! but yuh be tryin'," he said, finally. "Whut med yuh ack like that, honey?"

"A—a—dunno. Yo' eyes scared me. A—a scared muhse'f. A don' seem tuh be *me* when a'm wi' yuh, Sam, a seem tuh be *you*."

"Well, will yuh come walk wi' me?" he suggested. "A'll promise tuh do like yuh wants.

A know the pruttiest holler i' th' woods fur ten miles 'roun'. Will yuh come?"

"A'd love tuh come, Sam."

"Well, come then."

"But a mus' ax Mis' Gilman."

"Darn Mis' Gilman! You ain' no slave, a tek hit, an' she ain' yo' keeper—air she?"

"A'd ruther she'd know," said the girl, slowly.

"Well, cuss hit all, go tell her then," he fumed.

Tanis came back quite radiant.

"She says a ken go. She says ez how a ken fix us up a snack in this hyuh barsket."

While she arranged the luncheon hamper, he walked up and down, impatiently, whistling innumerable variations on "The Mocking Bird," but, as she came towards him in her pink and white sun-bonnet, with the basket over her arm, the impatience all merged into one vast smile.

"Honey," he said, regarding her delightedly, "yuh be that prutty a culdn't trust ole Moses his-se'f wi' yuh! Yuh be brighter'n a snake wi' a new skin! Yuh be prutty 'nuff tuh tu'n th' Devil interrer a Mithydist, an' a Mithydist interrer a devil. A feel jess like eatin' yuh up," and he clacked his strong teeth at her.

They walked along the high road to the Healing Springs, and then turned into Lion Gorge. The warm fumes of the May mounted to their heads. Their eyes shone, their strong hearts pulsed vehemently. They made excuses to take the basket from each other every few yards, that their longing hands might come in contact. Above them, the vine-draped rocks rustled against a sky of egg-shell blue. The torrent, at their side, swirled glistening among its moss-greened stones, and made the clustering cresses quiver gaily.

"Oh, th' spring be here!" he began to sing in his pleasant bass, and she joined to it her clear treble.

> "Oh! th' spring be here,
> Wi' th' green o' th' year
> An' th' wile turkey's gobble,
> An' th' deep crick's bobble,
> An' th' city folks a-comin',
> An' th' band a tum-tummin',
> An' th' fiddles all a-squealin',
> At th' Hot an' th' Healin'."

It made a good march, and they went on faster
than ever, now swinging the basket between them.

> "Oh! th' Sang's in bloom,
>   An' th' Sang-gal's at the loom,
>   A-weavin' her a shawl
>   Fur tuh war i' th' fall,
>   When th' Sang be ripe fuh diggin',
>   An' th' cider hard fuh swiggin',
>   An' we 'Snakes' go a-dealin'
>   At th' Hot an' the Healin'!"

"Yuh cert'n'y do mek up good varses, Sam," she
said, admiringly. "Why don't yuh mek a book
o' varses an' print 'em?"

"Sho!" he said, rather grandly, "them hain't
nuthin'. A ken talk varses like them thar easy ez
breathin'. A mought do sup'n' right good, ef a
sot down an' scratched muh head, though."

They had now reached the hollow, of which
he had spoken, but between them and its loveliest
nook stretched a brawling stream, over which a
pine tree had been thrown for a bridge.

"Ken yuh walk hit, sugar, or mus' a cy'ar
yuh?" he asked.

Tanis gave her rich, roaring laugh.

"G'long, Sam Rose! Ez many cricks ez yuh is ben see me crost! Why, a cud hop over that thar tree on one foot."

"Less see yuh, then," replied her lover.

"Well—a will," she answered. "Only a mus' yank off these hyuh duds fust." And, seating herself on the grass, she unlaced and drew off her stout boots, handing them to him.

"My Lawd, but ain't that good, tho'?" she cried, joyously. "Warin' shoes is like warin' cosits on yuh foots. Yuh dunno how good 'tis tuh move ev'y toe, 'thout hevin' 'em 'ginst sup'n' !"

With a cry and a leap she was on the slender pine pole, her arms outstretched, her muscular feet gripping the rough bark. He watched her, admiringly, but with some anxiety.

"Look out!" he called, warningly. "Don' th' water mek yo' head swim?"

"Naw, hit don't," she called back. "A feels like a wuz 'live fuh th' fust time in weeks. Shoes cert'n'y duz mek a diffunce in a bordy's feelin's!

Seems like a cud fly! Seems like, ef a hel' muh breath an' guv a good kick, a cud histe muhse'f right over that thar mountin'!"

She gave another yell of sheer delight and, flinging herself in the moss on the opposite bank, rolled about like a colt. Sam crossed somewhat more cautiously, as he had not taken off his boots. Then he stood looking down on her, with the proud indulgence of a man who watches the playful writhings of a young panther which he has half tamed.

"Tanis," he said suddenly, "yuh be a mountain gal, yuh be wile an' na'chul ez them vines an' things you're a rollin' on. Yuh 'on't nuvver git used tuh livin' onder a roof, Tanis. Yuh 'on't nuvver larn tuh walk easy in city duds 'n' shoes like these hyuh." He shook contemptuously the boots which he still held. "Yuh be free an' wilful ez that water yonder, yuh 'on't nuvver wuk onder saddle no mo'n a wilecat 'ud. Why cyarn't yuh love me an' give yuhse'f tuh me, and come back tuh the hills an' be happy 'n' yo' own way?"

Tanis, half ashamed of her outburst, was sitting

up smoothing her roughened hair. He held out
the shoes to her and she drew them on in silence,
but without lacing them up.

"A said a wouldn't pester yuh," he went on,
walking at her side, "an' a won't, but a do wisht
yu'd mek things clarer tuh me."

They had now reached the cascades. Walls of
high, firm-tufted rock cast a drowsy shadow over
the stream brawling between them. Far above
shone a strip of milky sky, against which were
outlined the dark green needles of pines, the delicate feathers of spruce trees, the young mealy
foliage of sugar maples. The boulders, lying in
the broad bed of the torrent, were vivid as with
soaked green velvet, and sunken among rich cush-
ions of cress.

Tanis leaped out upon a flat stone in the very
middle of the tumbling foam, and in an instant
Sam was close beside her. Their hands touched,
clasped, and thus they stood, gazing up the narrow
passageway of rock at the eager water.

"That's like muh love fuh yuh, honey," he ventured to whisper. "Hit's dark, mebbe, an' hit runs

rough, but hit's a-goin' tuh git whar hit's boun'
fuh, yuh kin bet on that."

"But hit's a-goin' tuh git smooth, too, arter a
while, Sam, down i' th' valley. Hit's goin' tuh git
out i' th' sunlight, an' run along peaceable an'
gentle."

"Tanis!"

"Yease, Sam?"

"'Ud yuh *like* a feller tuh be suh darned gentle
an' mealy-mouthed wi' yuh *all* th' time?"

"A didn't seh nothin' 'bout mealy-mouthed,
Sam!"

"'Ud yuh like yo' man tuh olluz ax 'mought a?'
an' 'moughn't a?' 'Ud'n' yuh like him tuh pick
yuh up sometimes—*so*"—he caught her up on his
shoulder—"an' run off wi' yuh—*so?*" He reached
the bank in a few agile bounds and sat down, keeping her on his knee, although she stiffened her body
rigidly and frowned.

"Be yuh mad at me, Tanis?"

"Yease, a be."

"Be yuh reel mad at me?"

"Oh, Sam, ef a on'y knowed how long yuh'd love

me, an' how much yuh meant whut yuh sez 'bout wantin' tuh want to be gooder !"

"A wants anythin' ez'll mek yuh love me an' marh'y me."

"But, Sam, marh'idge is like a cliff. Men's love an' wimmin's love is both gotter go over hit. But seems tuh me, ez wimmin's love goes over, like that water at th' Fallin' Springs—hit's all th' pruttier 'n' whiter fuh hit. But men's love—*mos'* men's love—goes over like a gret big rock, a knockin' things tuh pieces, an' a smashin' of hitse'f at th' bottom. Hones' Injun, a be 'fraid o' marh-'idge, Sam."

"Well, a'll tell yuh one thing, muh prutty, yuh be th' fust gal uvver *I* see ez a *wanted* tuh marh'y."

"Be a, Sam ?"

"Yuh be th' fust 'ooman uvver went tuh muh head wuss'n a drink. A b'leeve th' ve'y thought o' yuh'd keep me from freezin', ef a wuz lost i' th' snow. Now doncher think yuh owes me supp'n fuh not drinkin' furrer a week ?"

"Hit cert'n'y did mek me happy, Sam."

He put his arms about her and drew her to him.

" Now, yuh mek *me* happy," he whispered.

She trembled all over. Love and the spring were in her wild young veins, but her heart was as clear as a star. She put him, gently, yet strongly from her.

" A don' want no love-mekin' yit," she said. " A wants yuh to prove yuh words. A don' want tuh do nothin' ez Bill 'ouldn't like—'n' he 'ould'n' like this—hyuh."

" A said yuh wuz cole," he muttered, sullenly. She flashed out at him, pale and indignant.

" A'm *not* cole! Yuh *sharn'* say hit. Jess case a shows sense, an' 'on't do ez yuh seh, yuh calls me cole !"

" An' mean-tempered," he put in, grimly.

She pressed her lips hard together and walked away from him. He watched her cross the pine-tree bridge and plunge into the woods beyond. As she hurried on, dizzy with anger and disappointment, his mocking voice was in her ears.

" Thar's wile-cats i' these hyuh woods, but a don' reckon yuh'll mine that, bein' kin, ez it war ! "

She said nothing.

" Yuh looks tarnation prutty when yuh're mad," he then remarked.

Still she did not answer.

" A s'pose yuh thinks yuh kin lead me on, an' fling me off, as yuh pleases, an' a'll stan' hit 'n' go on bein' a damn whinin', slobberin' puppy?"

Still silence.

" Hyuh! yuh answer me, will yuh?" he thundered, laying his hand on her arm.

She shook it off.

" By Gawd! a'll *mek* yuh love me!" he said, hoarsely, with clenched teeth, and she felt herself caught and held, her head bent back, furious, scorching kisses on eyes, lips, throat, shoulders. She was a woman, although a half savage one, and she began to sob bitterly, but he continued to kiss her, until his mouth was salt with her tears—merciless, rough caresses, that bruised heart and soul, as well as body.

He released her at last, a very devil in his light eyes.

" Thar's not th' gal in Heaven or out ez ken play

farst'n' loose wi' *me*," he said, threateningly, but something in her stricken face awed him. He turned from her and stood silent, stripping the bark from a cedar tree nearby. Presently he felt a soft touch on his arm.

"Sam," she said, "a knows yuh wuz mad, an' jess a-tryin' tuh skeer me, an'—an'—a fuhgives yuh, Sam. Will yuh tek me back now? An'—an'—please don' seh much tuh me."

He looked at her, and said, curtly :

"Th' devil's in me, Tanis, an' that's all about hit. A'm a bad lot. A reckon yuh knows that, ez well ez anybordy. When th' devil gits up in me a cyar'nt down him. A hain't a safe man. A'm everlarstin' onreliable, but a loves yuh."

"A—a reckon yuh be right bad, Sam," she said, slowly, "but a'll gi' yuh another charnce. On'y tek me home now. Mis' Gilman'll be a-wonderin'."

CHAPTER X.

WHEN they reached the Gilmans' gate Tanis was about to enter silently, but Sam grasped her arm.

"*A'm* bad, Tanis, an' a reckon muh *love's* bad, too, but a'm agoin' tuh hev yuh, one way or-ruther."

She looked calmly up at him.

" Well, a reckon yuh done know me s'well ez yuh mought," she said. "Yuh 'on't hev me 'thouten a lets yuh."

"A *will*, though! A swars by th' tokin."

"A'd kill muhse'f fust."

"Naw. You mought kill yuhse'f arterwards, but not fust."

"Yuh cyarn't do hit. Yuh be strong, but supp'n i' me tells me *I* be stronger."

"But yuh loves me."

" Yease, a loves yuh. Mo' shame tub me."

He took her face between both hands and gazed hungrily into her eyes.

"*Why* does yuh love me, beauty?"

"Supp'n i' yuh draws me. Hit draws me like th' sun sucks up water—like th' drarff draws th' flame up th' chimbly."

"An' yuh holes back, jess caze a'm bad?"

"Thet's hit."

He smiled.

"Want me tuh tell yuh supp'n', honey?"

"Mh—hm."

"Hit's th' very cussedness in me ez draws yuh."

"Aw, no! *no!*"

"A swar 'tiz. Wimmins is like that. A bet Eve loved Cain a darn sight mo' nor uvver she loved Abel."

"He wuz her fust-bawn."

"That hain't nuthin'. She loved him mo', anyhow. Didn'n' yuh love that thar pesky leetle lame squr'l o' yo'n better nor all th' pretty beases thet Bill an' me uvver brung yuh?"

She moved restlessly.

"That wuz caze he couldn'n' he'p hisse'f."

"An' yuh thinks yuh ken he'p *me?* A've a

mine tuh tell th' stark-nekkit truth fuh onct i'
muh life."

"Aw yease! tell hit, Sam."

"Then spread them prutty years o' yourn wide,
fuh hyuh be a truth ez'll fill 'em chuck-full. A
loves yuh, chile, but yuh hain't th' fust a've
loved, an' a hain't got no cause tuh think yuh'll
be th' larst. A thinks *now* ez no har be wuth
lookin' at 'thout hit shines like a bay hawse in th'
sun, but mebbe, come a yeah, a'll be ez mad fuh
har ez is blacker'n a fresh-split lump o' coal. A
loves yuh so a hain't teched whisky furrer week,
but muh tickler's a-bu'nin' muh porkit now, an'—
mebbe a wone hole out another week. A loves
yuh, but a've got a 'tarnal thust fuh liquor.
Seems like a'd let yuh stick me like a pig fuh one
long kiss on that mouf o' yo'n, but mebbe, come a
week, a 'on't feel so no mo.' A tells yuh a'll
marh'y yuh, but a reckon ef a cud git yuh *'thout*
marh'y'n' yuh, a'd be moughty glad. Ef we had
chilluns a'd beat 'em, sho' 'nuff, a reckon, an'
mebbe a'd beat *you*. Muh love's right smart like
bar love, a reckon. A'd like tuh hug yuh twel

a kilt yuh. Ez fuh goodness, thar hain't 'nuff in me tuh mek a 'Amen' outer. Thar, a lay a've tole th' truth this time."

She was silent, and then said slowly :

"A'll gi' yuh another charnce. *Truth's* good, an' a lay yuh tole 'nuff o' thet thar, jess now, tuh 'amen' a book o' pra'rs. Now g'long, an' good night."

He went off, whistling rather thoughtfully, and she returned to the house, with the lunch-basket still full upon her arm.

Ten days afterward Alice sent her with some beef-tea and cream to the cabin of an old man, half way up the Warm Springs mountain. A pig hustled by her as she entered, and some hens were making themselves cosy in the warm ashes on the hearth.

The sick man lay on his back among a mass of rags and corn-shucks. She thought that he was dead at first, he was so still and waxy-white, his wide eyes staring up at a hole in the roof, but, as she came toward him, he said feebly:

" 'S'that you, Doc ?"

"Naw, suh," she answered. "Hit's me—Tanis Gribble. A've brung you some beef-juice 'n' cream from Mis' Gilman, i' th' valley. Be yuh in much mis'ry, suh?"

"Naw, a been't. A thought t'war th' doctor wi' mo' truck. Did yuh see muh Susy ez yuh come 'long? A be mortal thusty! Susy, she be a goodish gal, but she air too yorng tuh feel fuh th' ole."

"'Udn't yuh like a fire, an' thet thar hole i' th' roof stopped up, suh?"

"Naw! Let be, let be. A'd like a drink o' supp'n', though, fus'rate."

Tanis poured out some of the beef-tea into a cup, and he sucked it up with noisy eagerness. As he was drinking, the doctor entered.

"Why, Joe," he said, cheerily, after nodding to Tanis, and feeling the old man's pulse and forehead, "you're better, man. The fever's broken. You're good for twenty years yet."

"Yease, yease, a knowed a war better, soon ez them two greenish stars parst onder th' moon. A've been a-watchin' 'em fuh three weeks now!

Thet thar truck yuh guv me didn' do me a bit o' good; a'd a tho'd hit i' th' pig-trough ef yuh hedden' stood by an' watched me swaller hit."

The doctor laughed good-naturedly.

"So that's why you wouldn't let me mend that hole in your roof, hey? You've been lying here watching those stars."

"Yease, Doc, thet be hit. You're a moughty good man, Doc, an' we mountain folks sots a heap by yuh. But thet thar truck o' yo'n ain' wuth a rotten punk'n shell."

The doctor laughed again.

"Well," he said, "I'm mightily obliged to those stars for passing under the moon just in the nick of time. But where's Susy? Is this one of her friends, come to wait on you?"

"Naw; thet be a gal fum th' valley. A dunno *whar* be Susy. Ole folks an' sickness tuhgerrer be moughty hard on a yorng gal. A reckon she hev gone out tuh git a mou'ful o' fresh air."

"But, Joe, you oughtn't to be left alone, you know. I don't like to go away until Susy comes back."

Tanis came forward, shyly.

"*I'll* stay wi' him, suh," she said. "A'd *like* tuh."

"You're a nice, good-hearted girl," remarked the doctor, heartily, "and I wish you would." He drew her aside. "You mustn't tell him I said so, but that granddaughter of his isn't worth her salt. She's forever gadding, and if my son and I hadn't nursed the old fellow through the worst, he'd be dead as a door-nail by this time."

"*I'll* watch him, suh. Tell me whut tuh do, an' a'll do hit faithful. On'y a cyarn't stay but twel sun-down."

The doctor patted her shoulder, approvingly.

"You're a good girl," he repeated, "that you are. I'd like to know your name."

She told him, and then he explained to her what she was to do.

"Before I go," he ended, "just run to the spring and fetch some fresh water. There isn't a drop in the bucket, and he'll be sure to want some."

Tanis took the bucket and started down a steep,

weed-grown hill, to the spring. As she stood
still for a moment, to look about her, she heard
a low murmur of voices, and, stepping forward,
saw, in a pretty, vine-cushioned dimple just
below her, the figure of a man and woman.
All the blood in her body seemed to surge into
her throat. For an instant, she could not see
or hear. Then the man's words reached her
distinctly :

"Uv *cose* a loves yuh ! Whut yuh takin' on
'bout ? Ud a *ack* like a does ef a did'n' love
yuh ?"

"Aw, *Sam !* Then kiss me again ! Lawd !
Lawd ! but Grandpap ud brek e'v'y bone in muh
bordy ef he knowed hit !"

"Yuh jess lemme ketch him huttin' *one* o' these
hyuh sweet, leetle bones, an' a'd choke out whut
breath he's got lef' twixt muh finger'n thumb."

"Aw, *Sam !* Yuh be *suh* strong ! A ain'
nuvver seed a feller ez big ez yuh be ! An' yo'
eyes be bluer'n chiny ! Aw, *Sam*, a loves yuh !
a *loves* yuh ! an' a've hed muh chice o' fellers,
too. But they ain' none on 'em got they way

wi' me, savin' you. Aw, *don't!* Yuh huts me when you kisses me like that! *Be* a truly th' prutties' gal yuh uvver seed, like yuh said, jess now? A use tuh hate muh har tell *you* called hit prutty. 'Twas so black an' curly hit minded me uv a nigger's."

"Well, sot still an' lemme kiss th' curls out."

Tanis was quivering from head to foot, but she managed to walk quietly past them, rinse her bucket, fill it and return calmly. Her skirts actually brushed them, as she passed.

Before she had gone a mile on her homeward way, that afternoon, however, Sam overtook her. His eyes were lighter and harder than ever, his face pale.

"Well," he said, falling into her step, "a reckon yuh thinks yuh've done wi' me *now.*"

As was her habit, on such occasions, she made no reply. He tried another tack.

"When a feller's starvin' and steals a bit o' bread ev'n th' *preachers* ain' suh *moughty* hard on him. Ef yuh *will* starve me yuh'll hev to bide th' consekences."

Still no answer. He stopped suddenly and jerked her about, so that she faced him.

"Look at hyuh," he demanded, savagely. "Doncher know a'm a bad ky'nd tuh fool wi'?"

Her expression did not change.

"*I* hain't afeart o' yuh," she said.

"D——n yuh! A know yuh hain't! Thet's jess hit. Folkes, ole an' yorng, beeg an' leetle, hev ben afeart o' me, nigh all muh life. An' *you* now, a sprout uv a gal ez a cud brek i' two wi' muh nekkit hans, *you* dars me, an' jaws me, an' tormints me ez yuh pleases. But a wone stan' hit. Yuh hyuh? A wone stan' hit!"

"*I* ain' afeart o' yuh," she repeated, coldly.

"D'yuh think a loves that orgly hussy a Joe Simmons'?"

"A heard yuh *seh* so."

"But, does yuh *think* hit?"

She looked him steadily in the eyes.

"A think yuh done know whut love means."

"Yuh thinks *that*, does yuh?"

"Yease, a thinks hit."

"Why?"

" Why ?" she repeated, her voice suddenly loud
with passion. " *Why?* Caze even a brute-*beas'*
be true tuh th' mate hit's chuz. Even a—" she
broke off, laying her finger to her lips. The wind
was blowing toward them, and, on the hill-side,
among the juicy, waving ferns, a stag was
crouched, the doe beside him. The late sunlight
gilded his splendid antlers and made the doe's
white scut and breast gleam like spun silver.
About them glittered a gauzy swarm of gnats.
The doe's delicate head rested upon her mate's
shoulder, and he was gently caressing her throat
with his flexile tongue. A poplar tree spread cur-
tain-like above them, and among its whispering
foliage an oriole was singing to its mate. The doe
stretched her soft sides happily and gazed with
eyes of languid satisfaction—eyes brimmed with
that innocence of dumb creatures so exquisitely
touching to those that love them. There was a
sound of falling water, of wings, of the feet of
small, scampering creatures. The stag reared his
head suddenly and listened. In an instant the doe
was on her knees, her dark eyes big with alarm.

"Thar," whispered Tanis. "Thet *deer* knows mo' 'bout love nor uvver *you* will."

The wind had changed. It now blew from them toward the lovely creatures on their couch of ferns. In a flash they were up and away, bruising the wild-flowers to richer perfume, breaking the undergrowth with swift, sharp hoofs. The oriole flew after them, shaking the pale sunlight from its wings.

"*That* war love," she said, smiling at him, with white lips. "*That* war *reel* love."

A sob broke from her. "Oh, Gawd!" she said, lifting upward her clasped hands. "Why be mens suh bad? Why be a brute-beas' better'n some mens?"

Sam stood watching her, sullenly, half awed, half resentful. She turned to him again:

"Walk home wi' me," she said, gently. "A've supp'n tuh guv tuh yuh. Walk home wi' me, Sam, an' be ez kynd ez na'chur'll let yuh. Thar's supp'n ez a *mus'* seh tuh yuh."

They walked side by side, in silence. Once, glancing at her askance, he saw that big, slow tears were falling down her cheeks, but he hardened his heart against her.

When they reached the kitchen the last radiance of the sun was tracing distorted reflections of the landscape without in the rounds of the great brass and copper pans hanging along the wall. The branches of dog-wood in a brown-stone jug on the table were beginning to droop like the wings of dead, white moths. Sleepy peepings and cuddling noises came from under the wings of brooding hens. The cows were lowing to be milked, and the calves, penned from them, druned plaintively.

The girl sat down on one side of the kitchen table and motioned Sam to seat himself opposite her. He obeyed, like one hypnotized. For a moment she let her face rest upon her clasped hands. She was very quiet, her cheeks and lips colorless. One of the great copper pans on the wall behind her made a background for her head, like the conventional halo in old pictures. Her breath came slow and deep, and she paused often between her words.

"Sam," she began. Her voice faltered, and

again she let her face sink upon her hands.
"Sam," she then said, in a braver tone, "A *hev*
loved you, Sam, a *hev* loved you *true*. A fought
agin hit, but hit seemed like hit warn't no use tuh
fight. A knowed ez how Bill 'udn't want me
tuh love yuh, but hit warn't no use. A knowed
yuh wuz bad, but *thet* didn't stop muh lovin' yuh.
Hit seemed like a *b'longed* tuh yuh, same ez yuh
gun an' yuh dawg did—like a war part o' yuh, same
ez yuh han' war. A *knowed* yuh war bad, but a
thought a felt goodness in yuh. A thought ez
how a could larn yuh tuh down th' bad, an' lif'
th' good. A war like a mother wi' a lame chile.
A thought ez how yuh cud be he'p'd tuh walk
straight. A come down hyuh, tuh these hyuh
folks, fust, tuh git away fum yuh, an' then, leetle
by leetle, a got tuh wishin' tuh larn tuh be mo'
like 'em, mo' gentle i' muh talk, mo' kynd tuh
other folks, tuh know mo' 'bout Gawd. Jess tuh
he'p yuh, Sam; jess tuh know mo' *how* tuh he'p
yuh, an' mek th' good i' yuh grow, an' th' badness
swivel. An' a larned whut reel love is a-watchin'
them. A larned whut a'd felt tuh be th' truth—

thet love ain' jess *wantin'* ; thet jess tuh long tuh
kiss a man ain' no sign o' *reel* love ; thet tuh feel
yo' heart a-scorchin' in yuh, caze o' him, warn't
no true sign ; thet thar war supp'n' better nor
thet. Supp'n' ez 'ud keep yuh lovin' him jess th'
same ef he got crippled or sickly, or hed his eyes
tore out. Supp'n' ez 'ud mek yuh love him even
mo' ef he wuz tuh git sickly an' leave th' hardest
wuk fuh yuh tuh do. Supp'n' ez 'ud mek yuh
love th' ve'y *pain* ez guv yuh a chile o' his'n.
Supp'n' ez 'ud mek yuh know yuh'd stay a widder
fuh his sake, an' be glad fuh th' loneliness ez 'ud
give yuh peace tuh pornder on whut he war tuh
yuh 'fore he died. A larned all thet, Sam, an'—
an'—a larned tuh love yuh mo' an' mo', twell hit
war like a gret tree, a-growin' an' a-spreadin' i'
muh heart. Muh breas' seemed like hit war fulled
up wi' th' branches, an' birds seemed a-singin' in
'em, an' flowers a-blowin' on 'em, same ez ef th'
Spring war in *me*, too, like hit war i' th' valley.
An' a tried tuh larn *yuh* thet, Sam. Oh, a tried
suh hard ! But a cyarn' mek yuh feel thet, no
mo'n a ken mek you know th' tormint ez is grind-

in' me down now, this minute, ez a talks tuh
yuh. Mebbe supp'n'll larn yuh, some day. Mebbe yuh'll git crippled or bline, or—or—mebbe
some other 'ooman'll know better *how* tuh larn
yuh, caze 'tain' i' *me* tuh larn yuh. A *thought* a
cud; a used tuh seh to muh own heart ez how a
knowed a cud. But thet's done wi', now. Mebbe ef a hedn' seemed suh prutty tuh yuh, mebbe ef muh lips hedn' been suh red, mebbe—
mebbe—but whut's th' use o' 'mebbe'? Hit's
a pizen wud tuh use, in a sartin thing. Whut
a *knows* is, thet yuh done love me wi' reel love.
Why, ef yuh hed loved me fuh one week, fuh
one day, fuh one minute, even, yuh'd a *died* 'fore
yuh'd a kissed thet gal up th' mountin—yuh'd a
cut yo' th'oat 'fore yuh'd a tole her them wuds.
Oh, Sam! them vurry wuds ez yuh're fooled *me*
wi' suh often. But now hit's over, an' a *knows*
hit's over, an' a wants yuh tuh *know* a knows.
An' a wants us tuh part peaceable. A wants yuh
tuh feel th' ain' no spite nor meanness i' muh
heart to'ds yuh, nor to'ds thet po' gal. An' a
wants yuh tuh promise me supp'n', jess caze a hev

loved yuh suh true, but mo' fuh yo' own sake. A
prays yuh, i' th' name o' Gawd, tuh promise me,
Sam. Will yuh?"

She stretched out her hand to him across the
table, and fixed him with her dark, hopeless eyes.

"Yuh'll promise me, 'on't yuh, Sam?"

"Yease, go on," he said, huskily. The hand
with which he clasped hers was cold and moist as
her own, but neither noticed it. Their eyes were
deep in each other's souls.

"Then promise me, promise me——" Her
voice choked, and it was between thick sobs that
she said: "Promise me not tuh harm that gal ez
yuh war talkin' tuh, this evenin'. Oh, *promise*
me that! Somehow, a couldn't bear hit. Somehow," she could not speak, and, drawing her hand
from his, put it again to her face and cried bitterly for some moments.

The man sat like a stone. His teeth were
clenched. His eyes stared unseeingly before him.

"A promise yuh," he said at last. Then she got
up and came over beside him.

"A—a ain' got no fitten wuds tuh thank yuh

wi'," she whispered. He felt her draw back his
heavy hair and kiss him twice upon the forehead.
Then she went to the cupboard and took down a
bottle of cooking-wine and two glasses. She
poured some of the wine into each glass, and then
dropped into them ten drops of a clear, yellow
liquid, from a little phial which she drew from
the breast of her gown. For a moment she stood
still, shaken by a passion of silent grief. Then,
mastering herself, went back to the table and
placed one glass before him, keeping the other in
her hand.

"A—a wants yuh tuh drink tuh our good-will
to'ds each other," she said, "an'—an'—tuh her
ez'll mebbe mek yuh good, some day. A wants
yuh tuh drink tuh a kynd partin' twix' us, an' tuh
all we loves an' ez loves us. An' tuh Bill." The
utterance of her brother's name broke down the
last barrier of her wretchedness. She flung herself on her knees beside Sam, tearing the glass
from his listless fingers and pushing the one that
she held far from her.

"Oh, hol' me tuh yuh heart, jess once!" she

sobbed. "Oh, my Gawd! A'd ax yuh tuh kiss good-bye, but a'd seem tuh feel that other 'ooman's lips a-tween us."

He held her convulsively, and she clung about his neck with all the might of her strong arms.

"A *hev* loved yuh! oh, a *hev* loved yuh!" she sobbed, the pent-up bitterness and disappointment of her heart surging into one cry of utter woe. "Oh, my Gawd! a *does* love yuh!" And forgetful of all else, save that they were to part forever, forgetful of his treachery, of that other woman, whose lips had been pressed to his only an hour ago, she kissed him desperately, heartbrokenly, as women kiss their dead, or the grass that grows above the earth which covers them. Then blind, staggering, she groped for the two glasses and put one again into his hand.

"Drink! drink!" she said, feverishly. "Hit's th' lars' thing a'll ever ax yuh tuh do. Drink tuh all them things a tole yuh. Quick, like *I* does!"

Each lifted a glass, at the same time, and then set them together, empty, upon the table. They gazed upon each other, but in their pale faces was only the grim look that is left by sore grief or some mortal illness.

"Now," she said, trying to part her stiff lips, in a smile, "that be all, savin' tuh say good-bye."

She held out her hand, and he grasped it, just in time to save her from falling heavily upon the floor.

When she came to herself, the stars were winking in the dark frame of the window, and a chill wind stirring the white curtains, as with a ghostly life.

CHAPTER XI.

NEVER had there been a more exquisite day in the Warm Springs valley. The wheat-fields spread like wind-blown carpets of precious stuff, in which the warp was malachite and the woof silver. Spiders hung their jeweled webs from flower to flower. Young birds, learning to fly, whirred twittering to the ground among show-ers of loosened petals from the fruit-trees where their home nests had been built. Against a sky of pearl and turquoise the peach blossoms wavered, like morning clouds in love with noon. Here gleamed a meadow, azure from fence to fence with blue thistles; there dazzled another, white with ox-eyed daisies as with a sheet of snow. The mountains resembled the walls of Eden, all matted with the glistening leaves of the rhododendrons and its glomes of airy pink. Beyond them one saw, in fancy, the wide streams, shallow enough to let a fairy wade without wetting her gauzy kirtle, many-colored as a humming-bird, clear and

bright as though with floating stars. One imag-
ined the spiky palms, the young pomegranate trees
in scarlet flower, the oranges dozing among their
blossoms, the eastern vines, the lush grass, taller
than a fair woman, and swaying with fragrant tas-
sels as golden as her hair. White hinds with silver hoofs, like the hind of Diana, drank from those
waters. More than one pair of happy lovers wan-
dered under those palms and pomegranates and ate
unchidden from the tree of life.

At least these were some of the fancies that
drifted through the mind of Alice Gilman as she
rode along a lane overarched by blowing apple
trees and bordered by half-ruined stone walls,
which made her think longingly of Massachusetts
and its green, rock-roughened hills.

The mountain air had begun to tinge her clear
skin with pink. Her eyes shone and her curly
blonde hair gave a youthful look to the contour of
her face. She was even girlish in her blue shirt-
waist and brown riding skirt. Tanis walked at
the head of the lazy white horse. Her chestnut
braids were tied with black ribbon and there was

a belt of it about her waist. Her gown of white cotton gleamed with reflected lights, cast from the grass and buttercups over which they were passing, and which also glowed upon the mare's white belly. Tanis had grown thinner of late; her fine jaw was squarer; brownish stains darkened her under and upper lids, giving her eyes a liquid, wistful look, and bringing out the whiteness of her forehead.

"Where is it you're going to take me?" asked Alice, presently.

"Didn' yuh want tuh see th' view from th' Warm Springs mountin?" replied the girl. Her voice sounded listless. "Thar's a good road fum here."

"And is the view really so beautiful?"

"Well, yuh see," answered Tanis, "I'd think so, anyhow. Seems like a'd sucked muh vurry life from these hyuh mountins—like they'd bawned me intuh th' worl'. A reckon *I'd* think hit all beautiful, ef 'twar pintly hij'us. But strangers teks on over hit."

They were approaching a flotilla of butterflies

that dipped and reeled on the breeze like fairy air-
yachts, their wing-sails of burning orange, of
barred crimson, of silvery yellow, of rose and gray,
bearing them back and forth over knots of cow-
slips and wild honeysuckle.

"Oh, Tanis, how lovely! Do these beautiful
things come here with every spring?"

"A've alluz seed 'em."

"Do you know that their wings are covered
with little feathers, as perfect as a bird's plu-
mage?"

"No, ma'am. D'yuh b'leeve that?"

"I'll show you, some day, with Mr. Gilman's
microscope."

"Thank yuh, ma'am."

"Are you tired, Tanis? You don't look as
strong and rosy as you used to."

"No, a been't tired. A'm all right."

"You look sad, dear."

"A'm all right."

"Dear Tanis, if you were sad or in trouble,
you'd let me help you, wouldn't you?"

"Oh, yease, ef yuh cud. Thank yuh!"

"My life wasn't always happy. I used to cry every day, for many years. You look as though you had been crying, dear."

"Does a? A reckon hit's th' spring fever. Hit alluz tuk me down a leetle."

"Dear Tanis, stop the mare a minute. I want to tell you something."

Tanis checked the mare's drowsy amble and let her crop the grass, regardless of the green foam which tarnished the bit.

"Come here, Tanis." Leaning over, the tender-hearted woman took the girl's face in her hands and kissed the melancholy eyes. She smiled, but not merrily.

"They seh that's th' way tuh mek a *hawse* love yuh, ma'am."

"Well, I want you to love me. I do so want to comfort you. You won't tell me about it, and I love your bravery, but I know there's something on your heart. I can always tell, when I'm fond of people. I won't worry you any more, but I know that something is making you very sad."

"Yuh'se mighty kynd. A've larned tuh love yuh, tuh."

"Perhaps the spring makes you sad. I know it makes some people very, very sad. It used almost to break my heart, but now I seem to be blossoming and thrilling with every plant and tree. They used to seem to me like the flowers on a great grave."

"That's whut *I* feels. A tries tuh put muh mind on th' flowers an' grarss, but hit goes deeper down. A thinks uv all th' graves. Some full o' dus', an' some o' bones, an' some wi' leetle chillun an' gals o' my age, a-lyin' cramped in them narrer boxes, wi' thar eyes shet, an' thar han's restin' suh quiet on thar hearts, an' thar hearts quiet, too. 'Tain' death a'm skeert uv, though. Hit's livin'."

"And yet I can't imagine you dead, Tanis. You seem to me to be as alive as the spring itself, like a very dryad. Long, long ago, in a far-off country, where people built beautiful temples and palaces of white marble, and where the purple sea shone between the delicate columns, in that country people believed that a lovely young girl lived in every tree and guarded it. They called them dryads. You seem such a bit of nature that I think you must have lived in a tree, once, Tanis."

"Did they uvver cut down them trees, Mis' Alice?"

"Sometimes; then they said that the tree ran blood."

"Did they uvver bark 'em? Jess cut off a strip o' rind all roun', an' leave 'em tuh die, leetle by leetle?"

"I don't know. Perhaps so."

"A reckon they did. A reckon some o' them tree-gals died thet-a-way. Hyuh, ma'am, hyuh be a bit o' sang. Yuh wanted tuh see some a-growin'. Hit's got a right prutty flower—hain't hit? Supp'n like a Injun turnip. Wait, thar's a foot-pick in yo' saddle porcket. A'll dig hit up fuh yuh. Less guess wherrer th' root'll be straight or crookit. *I* guess crookit."

"Well, I'll guess straight, then."

The girl dug for some moments, and then tore

up the bit of ginseng, which parted from the soil with a crackling sound. She held it up.

"Yuh wuz right. Hit's straight ez a carrot. Marh'idge is right smart like bettin' 'bout sang-roots, a reckon. Yuh nuvver knows wherrer yuh'll git a straight man orrer crookit 'un. But *one* thing's *sho'*,"—she shook the loam from the web of tangled fibres, which spread like a net above the main root—"thar's alluz leetle worrits a-hangin' on tuh hit, be hit straight or crookit. Yuh got a straight, soun' man in yo' marh'idge, Miss Alice"—she had fallen into this pretty southern trick of addressing her mistress as though she were a young girl—"but yuh'se boun' tuh hev yuh worrits. What's suh nice, tho', is thet yo' husbun' takes 'em, an' meks 'em intuh sorter strings like fuh tyin' yo' heart tuh his'n. When a 'ooman hev got a husbun' like your'n, Miss Alice, a hole's ez how she ought tuh let ev'ybordy know 'bout hit. 'T'ud be right prutty, 'udn't hit, ef all them ez hed good husbun's 'ould print a paper 'bout hit fuh them ez hedn't to read? 'T'ud mek them others moughty sad, a reckon, but 't'ud keep 'em fum losin' they faith in *all* men folks. Hit's hard on a 'ooman when she loses her faith in *all* men folks."

"Yes, and it isn't right. The world is full of splendid, good men."

"Aw, no! You reckon? A reckon not."

"Yes, but it is. Men have môre to tempt them and make them bad, as a rule."

"Aw, no! A reckon not, Miss Alice. Hit tuk a snake tuh timpt Eve, an' a snake's moughty cunnin'. Hit tuk mo' tuh timpt her un hit did tuh timpt ole Adam, but she war timpted, though. Some wimmins is got feelin's ez strong ez men's, an' timptations stronger. But a 'ooman's na'chully gooder'n a man. She keers mo' tuh keep herse'f clean. Mens is mo' like pigs. Ev'n white pigs likes a bit o' mud. But decent wimmins. 'min's me mo' o' white pigeons. They like tuh keep theyselves clean. A dunno how 'tis. A ain't nuvver hed no use fuh mens, savin' yo' husbun' an' my brother Bill. Bill's rough, an' he ain't 'ligious. An' a reckon he's gone wi' wimmins, same ez mos' yorng fellers

is, ez ain' beases.   But Bill 'ud chop off his
right han' wi' his lef' 'fore he'd wrong a reel
good gal, or mek up turrer reel low-down one."

"You must miss him so much, Tanis, dear."

The girl's lips quivered, then turned inward,
firmly.

"Yease, a misses him."

"But he'll be coming back before very long,
now?" suggested Alice.   With that strong instinct of the tender-hearted, she felt that Tanis
was suffering intensely from some hidden mental
pain.

The melancholy eyes moistened.

"Yease, 't'on't be lorng, now."

They never could tell how it happened, but
just at this moment old Bess stumbled, tried to
recover herself, and fell heavily, pitching Alice
over her head into a clump of ferns.   When Tanis reached her she was sitting up, holding her
shoulder with one hand, and staring dazedly
about her.

"I'm not hurt—I'm not hurt," she said, over
and over.

Tanis was as white as her frock.

She lifted her mistress, bodily, upon her knees, and sat smoothing and rocking her.

"I'm not hurt—I'm not hurt," Alice kept repeating.

"A thought yuh wuz kilt," whispered Tanis, and began to sob. "Oh, a thought yuh was kilt, an' a *does* love yuh." She stopped sobbing as suddenly as she had begun, and felt the slight body that she held with soft, inquiring touches. "Done nowhar hu't yuh?" she asked, anxiously.

"No, dear. No, truly. I'm dizzy. That's all."

"Oh!" cried Tanis, still clasping her jealously. "Ef yuh hed a ben kilt, *I'd* a kilt thet thar ole lummux—a'd a knocked her i' th' heade wi' a rock, a wad! Oh, Miss Alice, tuh think yuh mought a gone, an' nuvver know'd whut a'se ben layin' off tuh tell yuh, time an' time agin, these three weeks! An' all jess caze o' muh own stupidness! A didn't know how—a wuz 'shamed. But, 'fo' Gawd, yuh is ben he'p Him save muh soul, Miss Alice! A hed a hard fight, but a won. A come down hyuh tuh larn, an' a larned. A

larned muh own *feelin's* were right, an' a *did* right.
Mebbe," she broke off, with a half dreading
modesty, "mebbe a thinks mo' 'n a ought 'bout th'
'provement a lays hev come tuh me.   But tell me,
tell me true, Miss Alice, 'ooman tuh 'ooman, done
a swar less 'n a used tuh?   Done a speak mo' per-
lite?   Done a ack mo' like a gal oughter ack?"

"You do, indeed you do," murmured Alice.
She was beginning to feel cold and sick.   "You
are gentler and more considerate."

"Bless yuh, bless yuh!" cried the girl.   "Oh,
ef a cud only go back an' teach muh people whut
a good feelin' hit gives yuh tuh *be* good!   Why
be hit, yuh reckon, thet th' higher up folks lives,
th' lower down they seems tuh git?   Why be hit
thet th' valley folks air suh much better then us
mountin folks?   Seems like thar *souls* be mountins, an' *our* souls be valleys.   But huccum a talk
suh much, an' yuh suh weak 'n' dizzy wi' yo' fall?
Hit's jess muh na'chul selfishness a-wukin' out, a
reckon.   Be yuh easier now?"

Alice stammered.   Her head fell back on Tanis'
breast.

"I—I—everything seems whirling."

Tanis gazed about in desperation.

"Mebbe yuh're a-goin' tuh faint," she said, "an' not a drop o' water, 'r 'nuff tuh drown a flea! Be yuh faint?"

"I should like," again her eyes closed; "water," she whispered.

There was a curl of smoke spiralling against the sky not far off. They were at the edge of a clearing on the mountain side. Tanis started. She had not realized before that they were near the cabin of old Joe Simmons. A clump of sugar maples hid it from them at this point. In an instant she had conquered her self-revolt. She withdrew her arms, and laid Alice gently back among the ferns. Fortunately, she could find nothing with which to prop her head, and the blood began to flow back into her brain.

"I feel much better," she murmured. "Not so deadly sick."

Tanis chafed her hands, and glowed with delight as a faint rose color appeared on the pale lips.

"A reckon yuh'll be all right now, an' ef yuh ain' narvous a'll jes run over thar tuh ole Simmons', an' git yuh some water. A 'on't be gone two minutes. Be yuh afeared tuh stay by yo'se'f thet long?"

"Oh, no," Alice assured her, smiling.

"Th' cabin's right over thar, a-hint them sugars. A'll run th' whole way, thar 'n' back."

She caught up her white frock and set off with the speed of an Indian. But neither old Simmons nor Susy was at home, and she had to climb in through the window, to get the bucket. She was afraid to bring only a gourd of water, for fear of spilling its contents by some mischance, and then Alice would have to be left alone a second time, while she went back for more. The spring, too, had been muddied by a cow, which had walked through it, after drinking, so that there was another delay while she stood waiting impatiently for the water to "settle." Indeed, luck seemed to be against her, for in rushing up the steep hill, her skirt slipped from her hand, and she fell over it, upsetting the bucket and soaking her feet. At least twenty minutes had passed when she returned to the place where she had left Alice and old Bess; but, to her amazement, she found that she had made a mistake, for neither Alice nor the horse were to be seen. Then she set down her bucket and ran several yards, back and forth, in every direction. The last time that she returned something occurred to her which, in her astonishment, she had not thought of before. She went forward and looked at the clumps of ferns, where Alice had been lying. Yes, there was the print of that slight body, but what was still more strange, the ferns were broken and trampled into the black mould, further on, as though two people had been struggling together.

CHAPTER XII.

AS Tanis stood, staring, something glittered up at her from the broken ground. She stooped and lifted it. Then her face blanched, and she sank to her knees, as though under a physical blow. What she held in her hand was Alice's long, gold hat-pin, with its little knot of enameled daisies cracked and crushed together, as though under a heavy weight. She walked forward mechanically. A bit of blue next caught her eyes. At first she thought that it was a flower, but, stooping, saw that it was the silk necktie which Alice had worn with her sailor-waist. Still further on, she found a little wash-leather glove and a bit of gray gauze, its frayed edges blowing like thistledown among the twigs of the thornbush to which it clung. Her face grew more haggard, her movements slower with each onward step, until, at last, she stood staring blankly at the wooded mountain-side before her, terror moistening her forehead and the palms of her hands, her heart beating loudly, suffocatingly, her body feeling as though made of lead. She tried to think, to guess at a solution, but, always, just at the same point, her thoughts veered and lost themselves in a dull maze of animal wondering, like the thoughts of an opium-eater.

Then, all at once, she turned and ran down toward the valley, as though a *wehrwolf* were at her heels. At the garden gate she met Gilman. He fell back speechless at the sight of her face, which looked stiff and chalky, like a death-mask.

But she sprang forward and clung to him, her fingers hurting him through the cloth of his coat. Her lips opened and closed—opened and closed—but no sound came through them. Then she darted from him and lifted her widespread hands toward the mountains. The blood had congested about her eyes and lips, giving her that horrible look, as though of clay. Gilman took one of the rigid hands and smoothed it between his.

"What's the matter?" he asked, kindly. "What's happened to you, child?"

She tore her hand from him and put it to her throat, as though in agony.

"Has anyone hurt you? Have you seen any horrible sight? Come, let me get you a glass of wine. Alice always has some Vin Mariani on the little table near her sofa."

Then she gave a hoarse cry:

"Alice! Alice! Alice!" She trembled from head to foot. "Alice!" she said again.

Gilman turned as pale as she was. He took her hand again and they ran together to the sitting-room, where, at this hour, Alice always lay on her sofa near the window, watching for her husband to come home to lunch.

"Where is she? Where is Alice?" he said, in a thick voice.

Tanis looked wildly about, then catching sight of the bottle of medicinal wine pinched out the cork and drank greedily. It seemed to Gilman that she would never stop.

"What has happened?" he asked. "Are

you mad? Where is she? What have you done?"

She went on gulping down the sweet, aromatic stuff. When she put the bottle down there was scarcely a drop in it, but she could speak, and the convulsive trembling was less violent. She told him what had happened several times before he seemed to comprehend it. Now beginning at the middle, now at the end, now recalling useless details which made him frantic, and upon which she dwelt with what seemed to him a preternatural obstinacy.

"For God's sake, make it plain!" he said. "Don't stop to tell me such things. What has happened? What do you think has happened?"

"Then," she began again, in a dull monotone, "then a foun' this hyuh pin. 'Twas daisies, jess ez na'chul ez them sto' flowers they puts on hats. Yease, then a foun' that. Then a foun' this hyuh leetle glove. Then a foun'—— "

He caught her hands and spoke to her imploringly:

"Tanis! Tanis, my girl, don't you see you are

maddening me? You said she wasn't hurt by the
fall from the horse. Then, what has happened?
Has she—has she"—his face was distorted—"has
she been killed, in any way?"

"Oh! wuss, wuss, a reckon!"

All at once she became calm, rational, self-con-
trolled.

"We mus' be quick, suh! You mus' rouse th'
neighborhood! You mus' ack in a jiffy! A reckon,
suh, 'twas sang-diggers ez done hit!"

She looked at him steadily. For a moment he
did not seem to comprehend. Then the light of
madness broke into his eyes. He lifted his hand:

"It's you—*you* who have done this! By God!
I see the whole thing! And you dare to come to
me with your cursed acting! You—you—!" He
staggered and fell back against the wall. "It was
you! . . . . It is you! . . . . It is you!" . . . .
he kept r peating. Then he roused himself suddenly, and she saw him dash off in the direction of
the Hot Springs on his own mare, a fleet, active
bay, with the marks of harness yet on her. She
stood, repeating stupidly:

"It's *me!* . . . . It's *me!* . . . . 'Twar *me* ez done hit! Yease, 'twar *me!*"

She went and sat in the kitchen window, as though stunned. She sat there until the mountains were dark against a pale, starlit sky, pulling the leaves from a shrub that grew near by, and shredding them in time to her own words: " 'Twar me— 'Twar me—'Twar me ez done hit!"

.   .   .   .

For a week the whole neighborhood, boys and men, scoured the mountains within a circuit of twenty miles. Even the visitors at the Hot, Warm and Healing Springs had joined the infuriated band, who, well armed and well mounted, were indefatigable in their search.

Tanis disappeared on the night of the day upon which Mrs. Gilman had been so mysteriously kidnapped. Old Bess had been brought home, a few days later, by a lad who found her wandering about in the woods, near Black Creek. As for Gilman, he neither slept nor ate, until the doctor, who acted as general of the little army, had convinced him that he would end by giving himself brain fever, and so incapacitating himself for assisting in the search for his wife.

They had spent a morning or two in hunting for the girl, but decided finally that this was a waste of time, as she had probably joined her gang and would be discovered when they discovered her mistress.

On a cold wintry night, more like March than May, a crowd of people had collected in the front hall or office of The Homestead, as the old hotel at the Hot Springs is called. They had returned only that morning to rest, while a relay had started off on what now seemed to be a hopeless search.

Several ladies had come down stairs to join their sons and husbands to hear the matter discussed. Through the cracks of the windows, built loosely for summer weather, the wind whirred and sang. The stove doors glowed redly, and the women had cloaks and shawls about their shoulders. They were even more impassioned than the men, in their talk of lynching. Now and then an appalled silence followed some dreadful anecdote of the horrible acts of tramps and sang-diggers.

It was during one of these silences that the hall
door opened slowly, and a girl stepped into the
warm, brightly-lighted room. She was worn and
pale, as though from a severe illness, her chestnut
hair hung in ropy snarls about her shoulders, and
she coughed as she drew her coarse brown cloak
closer about her.

Everyone stared at her, wordless, and she stared
back at them, also without speaking.

Finally, one of the clerks came forward.

"What do you want?" he said. "Who are
you?"

She said distinctly, but coughing between the
words :

"A wants tuh seh Mr. Gilman, an' a be Tanis,
th' sang-digger."

Then began an indescribable hubbub.

She was seized and held.

"'Tain' no use a-doin' thet," she said, gently.
"A reckon a come hyuh uv muh own free will. A
reckon a knowed a cud'n' git away."

The buzz grew louder and louder. The
women stared angrily at her, and whispered

their opinions to each other, and to their husbands.

"Yes, she cert'n'y does look about as bad as they make 'em," said one of the clerks, who was still grasping her shoulders, in spite of her very logical remarks.

The girl shivered, but did not speak.

"Mr. Gilman isn't here," said a gray-haired gentleman, approaching her. "He's out searching for his wife."

She looked at him wistfully.

"Who'd a bes' talk wi', next to him?" she then asked.

"Why, tell all of us." "Say what you've got to say here." "What's the use of telling Mr. Gilman in particular?" The voices rose and surged angrily about her. Involuntarily she tried to lift her hands to her ears. It seemed to her that these bright-eyed, eager faces were crueler than the faces of wolves.

"You see," cried the other man, who grasped her triumphantly, "it's just as well we held her, after all."

A hum of approval followed his words. Then a
young fellow stepped forward from behind the
desk. He had clear, widely-opened eyes, and a
frank face, with a kindly, boyish expression about
the mouth.

"Say," he remarked, "I'm going to wake the
doctor. He knows a lot more about these people
than anybody here does. I'd like to see if he agrees
with me. I think that girl is honest, and I think
she has got something worth telling, too."

A wave of crimson spread over Tanis' throat
and forehead. Her lips parted. A light came into
her eyes.

"Aw—thank yuh—*thank* yuh !" She spoke in
a whisper, but the young fellow heard her. He
gave her an encouraging nod, in spite of the angry
hubbub that had arisen at his suggestion, and
walked rapidly down the long hall.

In a few minutes he came back with the doctor,
a tall man, with shrewd, kindly eyes, and an ab-
rupt way of speaking.

He looked at the girl, stepped up to her, and,
putting his hand under her chin, lifted it so that

he could see her face more distinctly. Then he started.

"Why, you're the girl I saw at old Joe Simmons' that day, ain't you? And—" he felt the wrist and forearm of the hand he had taken. "Murder, child, but you're thin! You've been ill, or starving, or something."

She looked up at him. Her heart began to beat heavily.

"A hain't had much tuh eat lately," she admitted.

"Pore little thing," he said, and patted her cheek. Something swelled in her throat, but she would not cry. She pressed her lips together and lifted her head proudly.

The doctor turned to the noisy crowd about the stove.

"Yes, I'm with Charley," he said. "I believe in this girl. I believe she ought to have a hearing, and I'm going to prescribe for her. First thing a chair, then a milk-punch, then a few minutes to rest in, then to talk as much as she likes."

There was a murmur at this, but "the doctor"

was not often gainsayed. He made Tanis the milk-punch himself, and then stood by, smoothing her shoulder while she drank it.

"Now," he said, "say all you want to, and nobody shall touch you."

Tanis sat very straight in the wooden arm-chair that they had placed for her. Her hands rested listlessly on its worn side-pieces. The doctor had drawn back her rough, curling locks and tucked them behind her ears. Her moist forehead shone like a slab of moonstone above the dark shadow which veiled her eyes. Her lips were steady, her breast now moved with quiet breaths, under the blue stuff of her gown. She had the air of a primitive princess addressing an assembly of rebels.

"Fust thing a wants," she said, in a clear, firm voice, "fust thing a wants is tuh tell that a knows whar Mis' Gilman be at."

A murmur began, and she held up one chapped, but shapely hand. There might have been a sceptre in it, from its pose. Somehow it hushed that indignant hum.

"'Then a wants tuh seh, ez how nawbordy hain' teched a har uv her head—that she be safe an' well keered-fuh. She hev hed plenty tuh eat an' drink, an' she hev ben kep' warm. She hev hed a place tuh husse'f, an' my brother Bill hev kep' watch over her, same ez a dawg."

The murmur broke out again, this time much louder, and several men started to their feet. Again Tanis lifted her hand. Her nostrils dilated and her eyes were fierce.

"Wait," she said, "yuh'd better lemme talk."

When there was silence, she continued, quietly:

"A sed ez how a knowed whar she wuz, an' a *does* know. But thar's some promises a wants 'fore a sez anuther wud 'bout hit. Uv cose a knows ez how yuh ken send me tuh jail an' keep me thar fuh life, too, ef yuh wans' tuh, but thar hain' no tormint ez'll git a wud outer me, 'thout them promises, an' a wants 'em on paper, too."

Loud talking and even swearing now broke forth, but this time it was the doctor who lifted his hand.

"Namersense!" he called out, "cyarn't you

listen to the gyrl for twenty minutes? Hear what she's got to say, first, and then get as mad as you like. Go on, child."

Tanis held her head more regally than ever, but her hands now grasped the chair-arms with a force which whitened her strong knuckles.

"*I* kin git her back. *I* kin git her hyuh in two hours' time, an' ez safe ez when she went. But a wone do hit, 'thout a gits a promise, an' in writin', that nawbordy'll foller an' try tuh hut them ez hev kep' her. An' yuh cyarn' nuvver git her, nuther, 'thout me. An' ef yuh sends me tuh jail, yuh cyarn' git her, caze a've gin a promise, ez a cyarn' keep 'thout goin' back an' stayin' in her place. Ef yuh puts me in jail tuh night, yuh cyarn' git her, an' she'll wisht she war dead, too, 'fore mawnin', caze Bill hain' God-amoughty, though he do be gooder'n mos', an' tho' she'd nuvver be no wuss off'n she be now, ef hit rested wi' him. But thar's others." A quick shudder overran her whole body. "Yease, thar's others, an' ef yuh put me in jail tuhmorer, when she wuz back hyuh again, yuh'd be mekkin'

me brek muh wud, an' a hain' nuvver brek muh
wud, an' a hain' nuvver goin' tuh, nuther. So, ef
yuh wants Mis' Gilman back hyuh, in two hours'
time, yuh mus' gimme them promises, an' in
writin', too. Fus', that yuh wone go arter them
ez tuk her. Nixt, that yuh wone put me in jail,
whe'rr hit be tuhnight or tuhmorer. Thar!
That's all, a reckon."

Then began a general pow-wow. The men and
women gathered in knots, some talking very
loudly, some in whispers; the doctor and the
young clerk, who had befriended Tanis, consulted
together for some moments, but soon the doctor
began to be called for, from all sides. After
about half an hour, he came up to Tanis and
said:

"All right, my girl. You shall have those
promises in writing. We've sent for people to do
it, and they'll be here in a little while. I'll see
that they act square by you. But now you must
eat something."

"Naw, thank yuh—thank yuh, suh. You's
ben moughty kynd." Her under lip quivered for

an instant. "Yuh cert'n'y is ben kynd, but a cuddn't eat. A ain' hongry. A done want nothin'."

"But if you're going off on another long tramp, you must eat, I tell you."

Tanis looked obstinate. The curves of her lips merged themselves into a firm line, and she shook her head.

"All right, all right," said the doctor, "I won't force you. But look here, child, you can trust me, can't you?"

She smiled.

"Yease, suh; a reckon a'm right sartin 'bout that thar."

"Well, then, tell me, how on earth did you manage to find Mrs. Gilman, when the whole country, mountaineers and all, have been hunting for her so long, and couldn't get a trace of her?"

"A knowed a place ez th' sang-diggers knows. A reckoned she war thar. En she war. A reckoned, too, a knowed why they tuk her, arter a'd thunk hit over a bit. An' a war right. But Bill, suh, he didn' hev nothin' tuh do wi' hit.

'Twar one man ez done hit, an' he ain' harmed
her, like a said jess now.   'Twar jess one man ez
done hit, but th' others they stuck by him.   She's
safe, suh.   She ain' ben hu't by nonner 'em.   Th'
man ez tuk her, *he* didn' mean no harm by her.
'Twar tuh git me tuh to promise supp'n' an' a've
promised; an', now, ef they'll lemme go, a'll hev
her back hyuh by daybrek."

CHAPTER XIII.

A N hour later, the papers which she had demanded under her arm, Tanis went forth
into the dark, blustering night, having said nothing
beyond the facts that she came to tell, except to
the doctor and to the young clerk, who had treated
her so kindly. To them she held out her hand and
said : " Good-bye, an' thank yuh," several times.
Then she went out, and the door banged behind
her in the high wind.

A faint, white blur was beginning to spread behind the mountains when the eager watchers at The
Homestead saw her tall figure coming slowly down
the path that led to the Warm Springs mountain.
The grass was stiff with hoar-frost and the hillside
slippery. She almost carried in her right arm the
slender figure that she guided. The wind had died
down and a frozen silence held field and woodland
as in a spell. Snow, too, was beginning to fall—

snow, dry and powdery, promising deep drifts. The two figures advanced slowly.

Gilman had been out all night, but they looked for his return at any moment.

Before Alice had reached the piazza steps, however, the doctor had cleared the office of people. The excited hum and buzz of voices could be heard from the large drawing-room, which opened into the main hall. He had explained to them how necessary it was that Mrs. Gilman should not be excited, at first. He wanted, if possible, to have her in bed and quite calm before her husband arrived.

When she and Tanis entered the office, therefore, they found only the doctor and the wife of the proprietor waiting to greet them. Everything passed off without any commotion, and the doctor called Tanis aside before taking Alice to her room.

"Mrs. Gilman wants you to wait until she can speak to you again. She wants to see you as soon as I will let her. Sit there, near the stove. Nobody shall trouble you."

"Thank yuh, suh," said Tanis, in an even voice.

She sat down, however, by one of the windows and watched the day quicken above the dark crests of the mountains. The sky was clearing and the snow had ceased to fall. The "weather-glim" pulsed with changeful gold, now pale, like the petals of a crocus, now deep, like those of marigolds. A scarf of rosy lilac spangled with white morning-stars festooned itself above the band of yellow. As the sun rose higher and higher, it seemed to be revealing fairyland. The valley had been changed, by some cold miracle, during the night. Every tree and shrub and blade of grass was sheathed, as in crystal. The roses and hyacinths bent gently under the fine snow, which shone like mica. They were like lovely fairies, powdered for a court ball. As the morning breeze began to stir, the ice-sheathed twigs gave forth a soft tinkling. The sky was soon an iridescent globe above the sparkling white earth.

Gilman arrived and was taken to his wife's room. The guests and neighbors gathered again in the warm office. Still Tanis sat beside the window, her eyes on the radiant sky. Presently the doctor came for her. She followed him quietly, heedless of the whispers and comments that broke out afresh as she rose to do so.

Alice was lying in bed against a heap of pillows. Her husband knelt beside her, with both her hands in his, but the girl could not see his face. When he turned to speak to her there seemed to be a light upon it. Then Alice drew her hands from his and held them out to Tanis.

"I know! I know all! I know what you wouldn't tell me, dear. I have told him. He is so sorry that he ever doubted you, and said such cruel things to you. Come to us, Tanis ; we want to thank you."

Tanis came forward. Her face looked numb and pale, and she bent mechanically under Alice's loving grasp. When Gilman wrung her hand she said nothing.

"I beg your pardon from my heart. There's nothing too much that I could do for you, or say to you !" he exclaimed, vehemently.

"No, no, it's useless. Words are so empty," put in Alice. "Oh, Tanis, dear, I have so many happy plans for you. You shall learn everything that I can teach you. You shall stay with me always, if you want to, until someone comes whom you love better." She smiled, and pressed one of the rough hands to her cheek. Tanis shuddered.

"Why, you've got a chill, dear!" said Alice, alarmed. "Do call the doctor quickly, George. He is the kindest man in the world. He will give her something to check this cold at once."

Gilman sprang to his feet, but Tanis stopped him.

"Thar ain' nuthin' th' matter wi' me," she said. "That wa'n't nuthin'. 'Twar jess somebordy a-treadin' on muh grave. *A'm* all right."

"And will you forgive me?" he asked, with an eagerness that was boyish.

"Aw—yease, suh. Uv co'se."

"And you will come back with us, dear?" said

Alice. "We can begin to-day, or at least we can talk it all over."

Tanis shivered again; then she said slowly:

"A—a'm sorry, Miss Alice. A—a—cyarn' go back wi' yuh."

"Why, what will you do, then? You can't stay here."

"A'm a-goin' back tuh th' mountains. A done reckon a war meant fuh th' valley. A'm a-goin' back tuh muh people—an' tuh Bill. A loves th' valley, but th' mountains owns me."

"Tanis, I am afraid that is because I spoke to you as I did," said Gilman. "Isn't it?"

"Some," she answered honestly, "but that ain't all. A've med a promise. A *mus'* go. 'Tain' case a ain' grateful." She pressed her hands together and stretched them out to Alice. Her voice broke for the first time.

"Oh! 'tain' that, Mis' Alice. Yuh b'leeves me, don'tchuh? Hit ain' that, *'deed* it ain't."

"But, dear, I can't let you go back. Be reasonable. Mr. Gilman has really suffered over what he said to you, and you aren't hard-hearted, Tanis. You don't bear malice."

The girl turned away, but they could see her shoulders quivering.

"Won't you stay, won't you stay with us, dear, dear Tanis?"

"A cyarn'," she whispered. "Oh, a cyarn', Mis' Alice. Don't timp' me. A ain' nuvver brek muh wud, an' a cyarn' brek hit now. A gin muh wud, an' a *mus'* go, an' soon."

Tears began to escape from Alice's blue eyes.

"I—I thought you would come," she faltered. "I didn't think that you would leave me so."

The girl looked wildly about, as though for help. She breathed quickly. Her lips were dry and crimson.

"A've gin muh wud. A've gin muh wud," she kept repeating. A fit of coughing stopped her. The golden white flashing of an apple tree near the window fell across her eyes for a moment, and made her start.

"Thar!" she cried. "Th' sun's up. A mus' be a-goin'. Done say no mo' tuh me. Lemme go ez easy ez a kin. A done hit fuh—fuh *yuh!* *I* hed tuh promise tuh go back, 'fore they'd let *you* loose. A *hed* tuh do hit. A *hed* tuh promise. An' now yuh'se safe, an' a mus' go. Good-bye! Good-bye!"

She flung herself on her knees beside the bed, and gathered Alice to her breast. Her tears fell hot and fast on the pale forehead. Alice heard her strong teeth grind together in her effort for self-control. Someone sobbed. She scarcely knew whether it was she or Tanis. Darkness shut out that icy sparkle. When she came to herself, the doctor and Gilman were watching beside her. There was a strong smell of drugs in the room, and Tanis had gone.

As the tall figure of the mountain girl began to climb the foot-path, down which she had come with Mrs. Gilman at daybreak that morning, the people in the hotel office crowded to the windows to watch her.

They saw her pass out of sight, into the woods

above, but soon after a young artist called out to a friend :

· "Come here, Davis ! Look at that ! I swear that's stunning. It would be a good pose for a statue of Eve gazing back at the garden of Eden !"

Everyone rushed to the windows.

Tanis had climbed upon the prospect platform at the top of the hill, and stood there leaning on her rough staff and shading her eyes with one arm as she gazed back at the valley, which she was leaving forever. The wind, which had again risen, blew back and upward her dark cloak. Her hair was whipped into a fantastic swirl above her head, and under her heavy gown the outlines of her vigorous young figure cut sharply against the background of gold-blue air. For at least ten minutes she stood there, without moving, and then, turning with a gesture as of farewell, leaped down and was hidden from sight by the tangled undergrowth.

When she reached a maple, which had been

blown down during the past night, a man came
forward and joined her.

His blue eyes had the glitter of ice under their
bright lashes. His beard shone in the cold sunlight like gold wire, and his breath had frosted it
near his mouth, as with a sifting of silver dust.
He laughed as he put his arm about her, not
noticing the shudder which ran through her at his
touch.

"A got ahead o' yuh *thet* time, didn't a, honey?
A tole yuh ez how a'd hev yuh, one way or nuther,
an' a *done* hit, ain't a?"

"Yease. Yuh done hit."

"A reckon a'll have a time of hit, a-tamin' yuh,
hey?"

"A done reckon a kin be tamed by nawbordy."

"Well, yuh loves me. Yuh done tole me thet
thar. An' a man ken do mos' anythink he's a
mine tuh wi' a 'ooman ez loves him."

She withdrew herself from his arm and looked
at him with an expression which, to him at least,
was inscrutable.

"A *did* love yuh," she said, in a low voice.

"Even thet thar drink a guv yuh an' drunk wi' yuh, *thet* did'n' kill muh love fuh yuh. But," her voice dropped and again she shuddered, " a reckon yuh've kilt hit yuhse'f this time. A done reckon even hit's *ghose* 'll walk no mo'!"

He laughed, and seizing her in his arms covered her grave face with reckless kisses.

"A reckon yuh cyarn' he'p lovin' me, sugar, whe'rr yuh *wants* tuh or no."

She was silent, and coughed two or three times as her head rested against his breast.

"Hey? Why don'chuh talk, honey?" he said, shaking her gently.

"A ain' got nuthin' tuh say."

"Don'chuh love me?"

"A'll mek yuh a good 'ooman."

"But don'chuh *love* me?"

"A 'ont nuvver fool yuh. A'll ack squar' by yuh, Sam. A gin yuh muh wud an' a 'on't brek hit."

"But what *I* says is, don'chuh *love* me?"

"Sam, doez *yuh* know what love *is?*"

"Yease—hit's what a feels fuh yuh."

"Well, *thet* done seem tuh *me* like love. Mebbe no two folks loves i' th' same way, but yuh hev changed supp'n in muh heart. A done feel to'ds yuh ez a usetuh. A done feel to'ds *nuthin'* th' same. But a'll mek yuh a good 'ooman. Now gimme yo' arm. Somehow muh breath's shorter'n it use tuh wuz."

They went on climbing steadily for about twenty minutes. Then she murmured under her breath:

"Aw, Gawd! *stan'* by me! A done whut a thought wuz right."

"What's thet, honey?" asked Sam. "A didn' hyuh you good."

"A wuz jess sorter thinkin' out loud."

"Well, let's stop hyuh. A reckon yuh be tired arter all thet thar trapeezin larst night. 'Sides, a wants tuh kiss yuh some."

He sat down on a mossgrown stone by the path and took her upon his knees. She rested inert and listless against him. The sun was now high. The ice-clad forest flashed and shook forth thousands of little circular rainbows.

The branches of the spruce trees seemed to

smoke as the wind blew off the light dust of snow with which they were sprinkled.

From a hole in the tree under which Sam and Tanis were seated a flying squirrel and her young ones peeped, shivering. Icicles hung before the opening to their nest and snow had drifted in upon them.

A bird uttered its love-call, clinging with numb feet to a branch of rhododendron bright with ice.

THE END.

www.ingramcontent.com/pod-product-compliance
Lightning Source LLC
Chambersburg PA
CBHW022354020726
47500CB00002B/274